The Magic of *Harry Potter*

Essays Concerning Magic, Literary Devices and
Moral Themes in J. K. Rowling's Harry Potter

Daniel R. Mitchell

The Magic of *Harry Potter*: Essays Concerning Magic, Literary Devices and Moral Themes in J. K. Rowling's *Harry Potter*

© 2007 Daniel R. Mitchell

Cross Timbers Books (http://crosstimbersbooks.com)

ISBN: 978-0-6151-7282-8

Printed in the United States of America.

First Edition

The seven books of the *Harry Potter* saga are as follows:

Harry Potter and the Sorcerer's Stone (1997)

Harry Potter and the Chamber of Secrets (1999)

Harry Potter and the Prisoner of Azkaban (1999)

Harry Potter and the Goblet of Fire (2000)

Harry Potter and the Order of the Phoenix (2003)

Harry Potter and the Half-blood Prince (2005)

Harry Potter and the Deathly Hallows (2007)

Contents

Harry Potter Mania

Every so often a device, a book, or an idea comes along that so captures people's imagination that it becomes a fad, or even a mania. It's an interesting phenomenon that is sometimes difficult to explain. It isn't necessary that the focus of the mania be something extraordinary. Sometimes an ordinary thing becomes extraordinary simply because of all the attention it gets. The *Harry Potter* books have certainly captured the imagination of many, many people, raising the question of why they have become a mania. Is it because the books are very good, or is this just another instance of that strange phenomena of a public mania? Perhaps, there is something truly magical about the books.

Despite their widespread popularity, I had not read any of the *Harry Potter* books until the first six books were in print. *Harry Potter* has been promoted by the publisher as a children's fantasy story[1] about a boy wizard who goes to wizard school. Since I didn't have any interest in either books for children or books on witchcraft I ignored both the books and movies.

My attitude changed and I began to read *Harry Potter* as a result of the controversy the books ignited. I was browsing through the religion section in a used bookstore and found a book by Connie Neal, *What's a Christian to do With Harry Potter*[2]. I knew that there are some Christians who think the *Harry Potter* books are leading children into the occult and portray poor moral ideals. Scanning through the Neal book, I discovered there are other Christian writers

---

[1] I later learned that J. K. Rowling says she did not intentionally set out to write a book for children but simply wrote what she felt was an interesting story. The publishers (Bloomsbury and Scholastic) decided to promote the book as a story for children. It's hard to argue with success.

[2] Connie Neal, *What's A Christian To Do With Harry Potter?* (WaterBrook Press, 2001)

who do not believe *Harry Potter* promotes or encourages an interest in the occult and also believe the books express good moral ideals that are consistent with Christianity. That got me interested and I decided to read the *Harry Potter* books. I wanted to see what all the fuss was about.

Reading *Sorcerer's Stone,* right away I found myself laughing a lot and discovered that it was a very entertaining story, filled with satire and humor alongside more serious elements related to an archetypical struggle between good and evil. It wasn't at all what I expected. Although the book is mostly written at a reading level and in a style appropriate for young people, the inventiveness and complexity of the story makes it equally appealing to adults. Reading the books answered the question I had as to why these books were so popular. What I found is that the author, J. K. Rowling, is a masterful story teller and she has created a saga that is as entertaining for adults as is it is for teenagers.

I was also struck by the obvious reference to Christianity at the conclusion of *Sorcerer's Stone.* Harry's three-day coma after being attacked in an underground chamber, the rejection of the philosopher's stone as a means of immortality, and Dumbledore's explanation that Harry's survival was the result of sacrificial love point directly to a Christian message. It is not explicit evangelism, but is nevertheless an obvious allusion to the Christian gospel. Read abstractly, *Sorcerer's Stone* states: a person who has the blood of one who loved him enough to die in his place is protected from a death curse and brought back to life. I was surprised that others had not seen the clear reference to Christianity.

As I read the remaining books, I discovered that the *Harry Potter* books are not simply seven separate stories about a boy wizard. While it is true that each book in the series has its own storyline that comes to a conclusion, each book adds to a larger story. Together the books tell a single story in seven episodes, a saga over four thousand pages in length. Unlike some series books where you can pick up any book in the series and read it alone, to truly evaluate the *Harry Potter* books requires reading all of them in sequence.

I was surprised at how complex the story is and by the richness of the moral and ethical issues that emerge from the story. I don't know how much of this was intentional by Rowling and how much was just the typical artist's unconscious expression of her own experiences and ideals. Whatever the reason, there are a lot of moral themes in the books that can lead into interesting discussions. *Harry Potter* is not simply an entertaining fairy tale about a boy who goes to school to learn magic.

Like others who have been enchanted by these books, I want to discuss *Harry Potter*. My interest isn't motivated solely by the popularity of the books or by their possible importance as literature. The mania over *Harry Potter* will eventually subside, but the books will likely remain popular for a long time. These books may or may not end up being considered classics of Western literature, but that decision is one that must be left to future generations. I like reading books and discussing the books I read, especially books that I found to be interesting and entertaining. The books contain many different ideas that could be discussed. A discussion of the literary archetypes and devices used in the books would alone make for a long series of essays. However, my interest is mainly in moral themes, especially Christian themes, and how they get expressed in literature.

There has been quite a bit of controversy among Christians over the *Harry Potter* series due to the use of magic as a literary device. The critics claim that the favorable presentation of magic will lead children to become fascinated with the occult. In addition, the detractors feel that the moral themes in the book conflict with a Christian world view and are inappropriate for young readers. I disagree with both of these claims. The magic in *Harry Potter* serves a literary purpose and is quite different from the actual practice of occultists. The moral themes are definitively Christian, even though they are presented indirectly without reference to religion. However, the story is also complex, and may be too subtle, or too frightening, for children. An adult will need to understand the books and consider the maturity of the child before deciding if a child should read *Harry Potter*.

If you haven't yet read the *Harry Potter* books, it would be best if you read them before reading these essays. Of course, if you aren't sure about whether or not you want to read *Harry Potter*, perhaps reading these essays first will help you decide. In any case, I'm going to assume you know the basic story and I won't try to avoid spoiling the plot twists and surprises.

It's Just a Book

One of the statements often made about *Harry Potter* is that it is "just a book." The implication is that people shouldn't be taking it so seriously. That's a bad idea as there is no such thing as "just a book." Books are, after all, a kind of magic where the intent of the author is expressed through words, a kind of "spell" or incantation. That's not to say that all books are written explicitly for the purpose of influencing the way you think. An author can have the main intent of telling an entertaining story. Nevertheless, the author has a world view and will inevitably write that world view into the book at some level. It would be extremely difficult, and require an enormous skill as a writer, for an author to consistently express a world view that is different from his own. If the author is writing satire he may create an absurd version of a contrary world view in order to mock and deride it, but for most books, the plot, characters, actions and consequences of the characters will express the world view of the author. Reading a book exposes you to the ideas of the author and if we do not read critically we may absorb those ideas without realizing it.

The ability of books to influence us is expressed in *The Chamber of Secrets*. Ginny Weasley has found a book that appears to be blank, but as she begins to write in it, the book responds to her. Over time the book begins to take over her mind, and she begins doing things she would never do otherwise. What appeared to be a harmless, blank book turned out to exert a great deal of control over her actions. After her rescue, Ginny's father reminds her, "Never trust anything that can think for itself *if you can't see where it keeps its brain.*" To paraphrase, things that look brainless may not be trustworthy. A book that seems inane or trivial may have an embedded message that is not apparent until it seeps into our own conscience and begins to influence us. This episode of *Harry Potter* warns us to watch out for books that have a hidden immoral message. It also provides a hint that maybe there is something in *Harry Potter* beyond simple story telling. As Rowling stated in an interview, "I didn't set out to preach to anyone...I truly didn't set out to teach morals, even though I do think they are moral books."[1]

We can apply the same understanding of books to the Bible. The Bible may inspire some and make others angry. Some readers may get a great deal out of the Bible, while others don't get the message at all. But we would never say that it is "just a book" or tell people to not make too much out of it. We would always tell the reader of the Bible to read carefully and critically, yet let the book speak to you. The complimentary disciplines of hermeneutics and exegesis are taught to Bible students for this very reason. We want to make sure we don't read ideas into the Bible while also making sure we do see the message that was intended. If we don't learn to read all books critically, we can develop bad reading habits that can spill over into Bible study as well.

Some may still object that fiction is used for entertainment purposes while non-fiction is used to present important philosophical and religious ideas. However, myths and legends have been used for centuries to express moral values through storytelling. In the Bible we find that storytelling plays an important role in conveying great truths. When David committed adultery with Bathsheba, the prophet Nathan gets David to see the sin by telling him a story (2 Sa. 12:1). This short parable allows David to see the sin first in a fictional setting, and then realize that the moral applies to him as well.

The greatest story teller in the Bible is Jesus. Jesus would expound on the law and prophets as well as debate with the religious leaders. However, when Jesus taught spiritual concepts, he almost always did so in the form of a parable. In his parables, Jesus takes the ordinary things of life that his hearers are most familiar with and then adapts them to his purpose. When he was teaching rural people, he chose agricultural metaphors, but when teaching city dwellers he would switch to a commercial metaphor. This is the most effective teaching method there is. The teacher takes what the person already knows and adapts it to his use, helping the disciple see the principle through familiar ideas and images.

---

[1] Barnes and Noble interview, March 19, 1999, http://www.accio-quote.org

In the parable of the sower, Jesus tells a story that expresses the way we receive new ideas. Some hearers are like hard, compacted soil and will not allow new ideas to penetrate. Others are like stony ground that has insufficient depth to nourish the new ideas. Sill others are like thorny ground where other ideas and concerns prejudice the listener against hearing and applying the new knowledge. Only the fertile soil, prepared and open to receive, will bear fruit. This parable is told in regard to hearing the Gospel, but it is just as applicable to the way we read any book. We must read with a receptive mind, not prejudiced opinion, in order to gain understanding of what the author has to say. Storytelling gets us to engage our knowledge of the world and our imagination, our emotions and intellect, all at once, and in so doing makes us more receptive to the ideas of the author. In addition, the plot of the story creates a structure that helps us remember the elements in the story more easily than if the author presented a long list of items to memorize. Thus, storytelling is the most powerful way we have of conveying ideas to others.

With that in mind, the strategy I am using in these essays is to first look at *Harry Potter* as a literary work, exploring its form, archetypes, plot devices and characters in order to understand how the story is constructed. With that understanding, it is easy to see how the moral themes in the work are expressed. Once the moral themes are worked out, then and only then is it appropriate for us to compare and contrast the world view expressed in the story. We should be able to see if the story expresses a secular or religious world view, and whether or not that world view is compatible with Christianity.

A Rollicking Good Tale

As previously stated, *Harry Potter* is a very entertaining story and that answers the first question I had—why are these books so popular? Reading some criticism of *Harry Potter* you might get the idea that the books are popular because they deal in witchcraft and magic. Now that I see how entertaining the story is, I can put that idea aside as too simplistic. The books are fun to read, period. In fact, *Harry Potter* could have been written as realistic fiction, with no magic at all, and be almost as entertaining. However, using magic in a story gives the author the opportunity to be inventive and to create solutions to plot problems that might be very difficult or mundane otherwise. Although the use of magic does serve a purpose in *Harry Potter*, it is not the main reason the books are entertaining. I will discuss the magic of *Harry Potter* in subsequent essays, but I want to start with some ideas on why it is such an entertaining story.

You may never have given much thought to what makes a story interesting to read. Of course, you don't really need to know why in order to enjoy the story. If the author keeps you turning pages to find out what happens next then you can say that it's a good story even if you don't know how the author got you to keep reading. However, it's useful and interesting to understand why any story is entertaining. If we can find out what elements of the story are capturing the reader's interest we can eliminate a lot of false and shallow ideas about the books. More importantly, understanding the structure of the books can help us understand how the moral themes and characters are developed as the plot proceeds.

To keep out interest, a storyteller has to get us to care about what happens to the characters in the story. If we don't care what is going to happen to Harry and his friends we aren't going to read very far into the book. The characters must be believable so that when they encounter situations in the story where they have to make choices of how to act, their actions will relate in some way to what we experience in life. In so doing, the concerns of the characters can become our concerns as well. In a fantasy story that includes magical things that we don't encounter in our lives, the similarities with our lives are in the form of moral questions and personal relationships. In other words, we don't have to worry what spell to cast with our wand, but we do need to choose between harming and helping others. Believable characters also make mistakes in judgment, stumble around in ignorance from time to time, and do other things that are typical of real people. When the characters have to confront the common issues of human life that we face, we are more likely to be interested in what happens to them.

One way to understand the characters in a work of literature is to look at the use of archetypes. An archetype is an idealized character that serves as the basis for characters in a story. We respond to archetypes because they express universal ideas, situations, experiences, and personality traits that are familiar to us. In the *Harry Potter* books Rowling incorporates a wide variety of archetypes into the character of Harry. All of these archetypes together make Harry a character that we can and will identify with, even though we are not wizards in training.

As we learn right away in the first book, Harry Potter is an orphan. This is a very powerful archetype that creates a sense of concern for him. It is instinctive to want to protect children and when we read about an orphan there is a deep, possibly unconscious, emotional response in us. Harry is no ordinary orphan either. As we discover, his parents have been murdered and Harry narrowly escaped being killed as well. He has suffered a grave injustice that has left him an orphan, literally and symbolically scarred for life. We instinctively want the orphan to be cared for, but we find out that Harry is forced to grow up in an environment where he is not loved and cared for but is instead treated as a nuisance and embarrassment. The poor treatment of Harry by his aunt and uncle adds to the sense of injustice that we feel and that further adds to the necessary concern for the main character that is essential to a good story. How Harry can overcome the injustice done to him becomes an important question as the story develops.

Harry is also an archetypical "chosen one" who has a secret destiny he must fulfill, similar to the legendary figure of King Arthur. Some of the interest in the story derives from the process of discovery the hero must go through as he learns about his destiny, what it means for him, and what options are available to him that might change or fulfill his destiny. By following the character's process of discovery we vicariously live that same destiny. By walking in the shoes of the hero, we are exposed to the problem and possible solutions of life's greater questions. Who am I? Why am I here?

The hero archetype generally incorporates a second archetype, "the quest." A typical quest begins with the realization that there is some evil in the land. The quest involves a journey of discovery, through a perilous land or to a perilous place, to determine the source of the evil and the means of defeating that evil. A hero on his quest must show courage, inventiveness, determination, adaptation, and above all develop the moral virtues necessary to overcome evil. Each of the *Harry Potter* books involves a quest and the series as a whole can be seen as one large quest to resolve the conflict between good and evil and to conquer death. This archetype is a metaphor for our own journey through life. Realizing that the world is not perfect, and that we are not perfect either, we must find the source of that imperfection and overcome it in our own life's journey. We must come to understand who we are, why we are here, and what we must do to live a good life despite traveling across a land of peril.

The books also incorporate a typical "coming of age" story. Each successive book covers a year at school and we see Harry and friends go through various stages of adolescence. They must learn what it means to be friends and how to resolve conflicts between both friends and enemies. We see the first stumbling attempts at romance, the failures and successes as each character learns what it means to care about another person. The students must also learn to balance studies with entertainment, when they must follow the rules laid down by adults and when they can or should act on their own initiative. All of these (and much more in the story) are events that we must go through during the transition from childhood to adulthood. For young readers, the events in the story parallel what is happening in their lives while for adults there is a sense of nostalgia for past events in our lives. In both cases, the characters can represent, and even teach, what it means to grow up.

Realizing that the story is one of "coming of age" is vitally important to understanding the moral choices made by the characters. We should expect to see a lot of false starts, mistakes, and changes in attitudes as the story progresses. By the end of the story, the characters should be better able to choose between right and wrong than in the beginning of the story.

A good story needs a conflict between good and evil that creates tension and an expectation of resolution. In part, we will keep reading because we want to see if and how the good guys win and the bad guys lose. *Harry Potter* is filled up to the brim with conflicts of this type. There are conflicts between Harry and his arrogant foster parents, Harry and the bully Draco Malfoy, Harry and some of his teachers, and Harry and the Ministry of Magic to name just a few. The main conflict concerns the threat to Harry from the evil wizard Voldemort. This conflict continues throughout the whole series of books. In each book we gain additional information that explains who Voldemort is, why he is seeking to kill Harry, and why Harry, and only Harry, can stand against the evil wizard.

Voldemort is such an evil villain that we cannot help but cheer for Harry and his companions. The villain is another powerful archetype that provides interest and keeps us reading out of our desire to know how such an evil person could exist and what can be done to stop him. As the story progresses, we learn more and more of what motivates Voldemort towards evil and where his strengths and weaknesses lie. As the evil of Voldemort is explained, and a means of overcoming that evil is shown to be possible, we have a desire to see whether that evil will be conquered. Until the evil is understood, and the battle for good is won, the story remains interesting.

Along the same line, a good story needs a mystery or riddle to be solved. As we read along in the story, we gather clues that allow us to solve the riddle. That stimulates the imagination, forces us to use our reason, and keeps us reading so that we get more clues. In *Harry Potter* we follow along with Harry, gathering clues and trying to understand how they fit together. A great deal of the story is spent investigating the riddle of Voldemort and his attack on Harry. As each story progresses, we learn more and more of the backstory on

Voldemort. Each clue, however, opens up more questions and the story often grows in mystery as you move along.

Rowling makes excellent use of misdirection in the story as well. Just when is seems the mystery is solved, some previously insignificant piece of information comes into focus and we have to reevaluate the solution to the mystery. These unexpected twists along the road to solving the mystery are another key ingredient in any good story.

It also helps if the story is set in some exotic location. We often have a desire to visit interesting places, explore different cultures, or just get away from the ordinary for a while. A good story creates a venue that is someplace we might like to go, but may not be able to get to except in books. A "magical kingdom" is certainly a place like that and is a typical feature of fantasy stories. The author can create a location that is a place we can never otherwise visit, but by using our imagination we can experience that strange and unusual place.

Typically, fantasy stories take place in a world that is completely different from our own. However, in *Harry Potter* we encounter a world that is a blend of realism and invention. That little twist adds an element of surprise within familiarity. We read about the typical things of our world, such as cars and trains and buses, but then, in the middle of that normality, fantastical elements emerge. Additional tension and interest in the story comes as a result of the wizards having to hide their existence from the Muggles who live side by side with them. By creating a world that contains this mixture, Rowling has the opportunity to directly satirize and comment on our world while simultaneously treating the world we live in as a mystical place with secret locations and unseen mysteries hidden just out of view. She has turned our own world into a magical kingdom, and done it so well there is a temptation to start looking for the hidden passageway into Diagon Alley.

Humor is another element that can make a story interesting to read. The occasional joke, pun or awkward situation that makes us laugh adds another dimension to a story. *Harry Potter* is sprinkled liberally with various levels of humor. Some of it is very juvenile, entertaining to children but typically leaving adults groaning. Who would ever want to risk eating a vomit flavored jelly bean? Yuck.

But we can also chuckle at the typical teenage behavior displayed in such scenes as the young boys drooling over the newest flying broom in the store window, or Harry's purchase of every item on the candy cart.

Many of the place and character names provide comic relief as well. In some cases the humor is subtle and you have to read the words out loud to get the joke. It took me some time to realize that Diagon Alley is a word play on diagonally, a clever reference to the hidden nature of the wizard's private spaces. Likewise, figuring out the Latin terms in the charms and spells, and the veiled references in the names of many of the characters, adds humor and interest to the story.

Mixed in with the silly humor and puns are many satirical and sarcastic comments on elements of everyday life. The Dursley's middle class obsession with social appearances, the bumbling, interfering politicians at the Ministry of Magic, the incompetent divination teacher and boring history professor at Hogwarts, and the journalists that print rumor and slander in place of true fact, all cause us to nod the head and laugh in recognition of the often tragic yet comic failings of human nature.

Finally, a good story will cause us to reflect on the issues of life that we all have questions and opinions about. Seeing a character face a moral choice, make a decision and have to accept the consequences of that decision, leads us to compare our views and decisions with those of the characters. It is not necessary or even desirable for the characters to be perfect models of behavior. The same moral questions arise, and we must consider the possible choices, whether or not the characters in the story make the right choice. Thinking about the choices the characters made, we can consider what we might have done in the same situation, and whether or not we think the author's choice for the characters is the right one. We may not agree with the author's perspective, but it is often interesting to read the story in order to get a different opinion that we might not otherwise have considered.

Taking all of these elements into consideration, it is easy to see why the *Harry Potter* books are so popular and entertaining. Harry is an orphan who has suffered an injustice and thus we can easily be concerned about him. There is a conflict between good and evil and a mystery to be solved as well. As Harry matures during subsequent years at Hogwarts, he faces the typical problems of adolescence while constantly fighting against the evil directed at him. He must continually face moral decisions that could affect not only his own wellbeing, but also the wellbeing of his friends, fellow students and teachers. As we read Harry's story we can think about how we might have responded to those same challenges. All of these elements together make for a very complex, yet entertaining and compelling story.

The Magic of Words

Harry Potter is not only popular, it is also controversial. One of the controversies surrounding the *Harry Potter* books concerns the use of magic. As a young wizard, Harry is enrolled in a school where he and his fellow students study transfiguration, charms, spells, potions and divination. They fly on brooms, travel by flying cars and a network of fireplace flues. Magic in the stories is used by both the heroes and the villains, although there are some differences in how and why magic is used by each.

The detractors claim that the use of magic in the story promotes and encourages an unhealthy interest in children towards occult practices. Some have even gone so far as to claim the books are a practical textbook for learning occult practices. Others will admit that the magic in the story is made-up, but feel that it is so intriguing to children that they will seek out real information about the occult as a result. Critics also claim that the use of the same magic by both good and evil characters implies that occult practices are not inherently evil, only evil in their use. On the other side of the debate are those that claim these are merely literary devices, purely mechanical, have nothing to do with occult practices, and are therefore harmless. Both sides of the argument quote heavily from the books to prove their respective positions. So, who is right and who is wrong?

Unfortunately, there is no easy way to resolve this controversy. You might think that a book either does or doesn't promote the occult, that one side of the debate is right and the other wrong. That is too simplistic, however. Interpretation of literature is not as easy as it may seem to be. The words, characters and events in any book, but especially in a work of fantasy, may or may not have a hidden or allegorical meaning. Where and how you attach a symbolic meaning to an element of the story can significantly change the meaning of the story. Likewise, just because a book talks about magic doesn't tell you very much about what the magic in the book implies. You have to decide if the magic is purely literary or contains veiled references to things in the real world. That is a matter of interpretation and involves attaching the pre-existing knowledge of the reader to elements in the story. Although we may not be able to reconcile the differences of opinion, we can come to understand why this controversy exists.

As I am fond of saying, "Words are a funny thing."[1] Any given word can have a variety of meanings and usage. We typically have to discriminate between different meanings of a word by considering the context in which the word is used. For example, "ball" means one thing in reference to sports and something entirely different if we are talking about dancing. Furthermore, any word both denotes (stands in place of something) and has a connotation. We think of a "ballroom" as something fancy and associated with formal dances, but a "disco" as something more mundane and informal, even though both refer to a place where people dance. Some words may even call to mind a complex set of associated ideas. Put another way, when we read a word we form mental associations that are not explicitly stated in the word itself. Because a single word can call to mind a large set of associated ideas, we may read additional meanings into a word whether or not we are consciously aware of doing so.

Words like "witchcraft" and "sorcery" have different meanings and associations depending on the context. In many instances, the word witchcraft calls up the image of fairy tale stories such as Cinderella, Snow White, or Sleeping Beauty. In that usage, witchcraft simply refers to make-believe elements of a story and doesn't have anything to do with reality. At other times, we use the word witchcraft in the sense of an ancient superstition and associate the word with unscientific ignorance. In still other situations, witchcraft may be used metaphorically, as when we say a man is "bewitched" by a beautiful woman. None of these usages have anything to do with the occult and there is no connotation of something inherently corrupt or evil. However, in other instances we

---

[1] This is, of course, grammatically incorrect. That's part of the "funny thing" about words. Violating normal usage can add another dimension to meaning.

use the word witchcraft in reference to occult practices or demonic influences. The connotation in that case is very negative. This connotation is especially strong for people who have had personal experience in the occult, spend a great deal of time studying the occult, or simply have a Biblical world-view. Those with a different background or world-view are much more likely to see the magic in the story as merely entertaining and inventive.

Reading hidden meanings into words is a key aspect of occult practice. The occultists give a hidden, or esoteric, meaning to words, objects and events in addition to the normal, or exoteric, meaning. A person who has been involved in the occult, or made an in-depth study of occult practice has already developed the habit of reading these hidden meanings. It is not surprising then that most of those who see occult meanings in *Harry Potter* are people who have extensive knowledge of the occult. Their association of witchcraft with the occult is so ingrained that it is difficult for them to see any other association. Despite their claims, this expertise is as much of a hindrance as a benefit. They are far more likely to read in symbolic meanings where they do not actually exist, especially if the words or objects are similar to those used in occult writings.

Although we should just let the story speak for itself without trying to read associations into *Harry Potter*, that's almost impossible to do because of the eclectic nature of the writing combined with the strong associations that people have with words such as magic and witchcraft. The conflict we are trying to resolve involves not just what is in the book but also what is in the mind of the reader of the book. To better understand this, we have to consider some aspects of human psychology and perception.

There is always a temptation to think that facts are just out there in the world and that we can objectively observe them and rationally draw definitive conclusions from those facts. The idea that "reality" is as much in the mind as in the world will seem strange to those who have never thought about it. However, we carry in the mind a set of assumptions about the world and those assumptions filter our observations while also acting as premises for our reasoning. As a trivial example, would you say the presence of a policeman on a nearby street corner is a good thing or a bad thing? A criminal seeing a policeman on the street corner might become very nervous, while an honest citizen would likely experience a feeling of safety. In more extreme examples, we might not even see something right in front of us because we are not expecting to see it. Anyone who has had to search for a set of misplaced car keys has probably experienced this first hand. Although the keys are in plain sight we don't see them because they are not where we expect them to be.

In addition, there are personality differences that affect the mental process we use in evaluating facts and making decisions. Some people are what psychologists call "judging" in their decision making. They will make associations, eliminate alternatives and quickly reach a judgment based on previous knowledge and experience. A person of this type will likely reach a conclusion about magic by the end of the first *Harry Potter* book and then use that conclusion to interpret the remaining books. Consequently, any later information that conflicts with the initial assessment will be either misinterpreted or ignored, making it very difficult to get the person to change his mind.

Other personality types are described as "probing" and have a preference for withholding interpretation until as many possible options as can be found are considered. They will want to read far into the books and use much more of the story in making a decision on questions like the use of magic and its potential meaning in and out of the story. Furthermore, a probing type personality is more likely to allow the magic in the books to be unique to the books and not associated with anything else. In extreme cases, the probing personality type may appear ambivalent or unconcerned, while the judging type may seem rigid and obstinate in his thinking.[2]

In philosophical terms, acquiring knowledge involves questions of epistemology and semiotics. How do we know what we know? How much of the knowledge we have is based on objective observation as opposed to prejudices, limitations of perception and reasoning, and other internal mental activity? It is entirely possible that the limits of human perception, thinking and communication can allow different people to hold very different viewpoints without either viewpoint being correct or incorrect in an absolute, objective sense. For example, two observers on opposite sides of an object can

---

[2] A good introduction of the differences in personality and how they affect the way we think can be found in the book *Please Understand Me II*, by David Kiersey.

both accurately describe what they see even though their descriptions will be different due to each observer's limited field of view. We can also arrive at a wrong conclusion because we do not have all the facts. Given the facts available we make the best possible explanation, but when additional facts become available we may need to change our explanation. However, even when those additional facts are made available, we may reject them as false because we have already formed a mental model that excludes them.

Another way to understand this epistemological problem is to look at the differences between "objective" and "subjective" aspects of knowledge. For example, suppose I take a chair and turn it upside down. Is it still a chair? In an objective sense, the same material and form are present and thus we would say it is still a chair. But in a subjective sense I can no longer sit on the object so the answer would be no. Likewise, is an antique chair in a museum display a "chair" or an "*object d'art*" since I am not allowed to climb up and sit on it? Looking at the object, we say that we are looking at a chair, but in actuality the material we are looking at is wood, metal, etc. A chair is an abstraction that exists in the mind, not the physical thing. We see the "wood" as a "chair" because it is in a form that we can potentially sit on. We can think of a chair objectively and define it only as material in a certain form. Or, we can think of it subjectively and only call an object a chair if it is something I can actually sit on. We can go one step further and consider a painting of a chair. We still identify the object in the painting as a chair, but it is actually a mere representation and nothing of the material or use of a chair remains, only the visible form. All this talk of chairs is not just some form of sophistry or philosophical "playing around with words." At each stage of change of material, form or context we get farther from or closer to the useful form and the object has varying associations with the abstract idea of a chair. Yet, we use the identical word in all cases.

A similar thing happens when we take something and use it in a work of fiction. The context and the form changes, and this can be considered a change in use. This goes right to the heart of the controversy over *Harry Potter*. For some people, the mere fact that the magic is incorporated into a fictional story is sufficient to remove any occult reference. That is, the context has changed and therefore the potential use as something occult is eliminated. For others, a change in form of the magic from that used in actual occult practice is sufficient to avoid an implication of occultism. But, for some, the word itself is what is important and any reference at all to witchcraft will be considered a reference to the occult.

This conflict between observed facts and preconceived ideas in the mind becomes especially problematic when we are dealing with potentially symbolic language such as that used in allegorical literature. In the case of a classic allegory such as John Bunyon's *The Pilgrim's Progress*, the allegory is easy to see due to the use of names such as Christian, Faithful, Hopeful, etc. When the metaphors are not obvious, it is not so easy to establish the allegory or to even be sure that an allegorical meaning is intended. For example, the headmaster of Hogwarts is named Dumbledore, an Old English word for a bumblebee. The bumblebee can be used as a symbol of some character trait, or it could be a hidden reference to some other symbolic use of bumblebees, but it could also be used just because "Dumbledore" is an interesting word. That leaves open the question of whether or not we should try to read some symbolism into the name of the headmaster. In this case we know the answer because the author has explicitly stated why she used that name. Rowling stated that the name Dumbledore "seemed to suit the headmaster, because one of his passions is music and I imagined him walking around humming to himself."[3]

When the allegory is not explicit, the reader must supply the metaphor to the story in order to read it as allegory. If we do apply symbolic meaning to a word, device or character, we have to be aware that we may be supplying the symbolism to the story from our own minds. The danger, then, is that someone who tends to read symbolic meanings into words may very easily read them into a story when it is not appropriate to do so. If a word or object is used in the story that has a well-known association, the temptation is even stronger.

Desire and how it affects our perceptions is one of the themes in *Harry Potter*. In *The Sorcerer's Stone* the mysterious "Mirror of Erised" plays a key role in the plot. In case you didn't notice, "Erised" is "Desire" spelled backwards. As the reversed inscription on the mirror states, "I show not your face but your heart's desire."

---

[3] Barnes and Noble interview, March 19, 1999, http://www.accio-quote.org

When Dumbledore finds Harry staring into the mirror he warns him, "this mirror will give us neither knowledge or truth. Men have wasted away before it, entranced by what they have seen, or been driven mad, not knowing if what it shows is real or even possible." In many ways, a work of literature can become like the "Mirror of Erised." We often see in a story what we desire to see, but a mere reflection of our own desires does not give us knowledge or truth. If we want to get to the truth about a story, we have to put aside preconceptions and let the story speak for itself. That requires that we start with a literary assessment of the book and not a prejudiced response to the words that are used.

The eclectic and complex writing in *Harry Potter* combined with the various meanings attached to words like "witchcraft" are the primary reasons for all this debate. The story has so many ideas and archetypical images embedded in it that a reader or reviewer can extract the part they find interesting and then use *Harry Potter* as a starting point for discussion. That diversity is also part of the appeal of the books. Because there are so many elements to the story, the books can appeal to a broad range of readers and be used to initiate discussion of a wide variety of topics. Rowling has created an amazing literary cafeteria where the reader can pick and choose the items that are most interesting while leaving the rest behind and still have a full plate of ideas to chew on.

To those who would debate *Harry Potter*, I suggest that you consider this carefully. Rowling has given you a book that you can use to talk about the things you want to talk about. But this is equally true of those who hold an opposite view. Each has seen in the books references to issues that are of concern and can use the books as a starting point for discussion. This is part of the true "magic" of *Harry Potter*.

Fantasy and Reality

A work of fiction, in one way or another, represents the realities of the historical period the author lives in. After all, an author must ultimately write about what he knows and has experienced. This is true of any historical period. We can see the ancient Greek world in Homer, Medieval Europe in Chaucer and Dante, and Victorian England in Dickens. Literature can show us the structures of everyday life such as social relationships, architecture, technology, commerce, religion, politics and even geography. In addition, literature will express the prevalent ideologies of the period in which it was written. There may be more than one ideology in competition at the time, and the author may only express one particular viewpoint. Nevertheless, when we look at any work of literature we see a reflection of the age in which it was written.

It may seem like a strange idea at first, but this reflection of our world by literature is every bit as present in fantasy stories as it is in realistic fiction. There is a major difference between the two, but what both realism and fantasy share in common is the ability to express the world-view of the age in some abstract form. Where they differ is in the objects, characters and places of the story. Realism in fiction must limit itself to using the actual things of our world. Although any author has some artistic license that will allow him to alter everyday objects and real places, there is a limit to how far the author can get from the actual attributes of real things before the story becomes unbelievable to the reader. However, in a fantasy story the writer can invent or adapt places, people and objects and incorporate them into the story without concern for conflict with the real world. As long as the places and things are consistent within the context of the story, the reader will be able to accept them without objection.

Thus, one of the advantages of fantasy literature is that the author can invent any form of magic he desires in order to add interest or help the story's plot. Because the magic is always invented to some extent, and the magic in one story may be completely different from the magic in another, the magic in each work of fantasy has to be considered on its own. For example, in *A Wizard of Earthsea*, by Ursula K Le Guin, a young boy discovers he has an ability to do magic and subsequently goes to a wizard's school to improve his knowledge. That story beginning is similar to *Harry Potter,* but beyond that slight similarity the two works have almost nothing in common. The magic in *Earthsea* is very different than the magic in *Harry Potter* and the events of the stories take place in very different worlds.

In addition to inventing magic, an author can borrow ideas from other writers and adapt them to his own stories. Part of what is interesting about *Harry Potter* is that Rowling borrows terminology, creatures and magical devices from so many other sources and then blends her own inventions in with them. As Rowling has stated,

> "[L]et's say ninety-five percent, at least, of the magic in the books, is entirely invented by me. And I've used things from folklore, and I've used bits of what people used to believe worked, magically, just to add a certain flavor — but I've always twisted them to suit my own ends; I mean I've taken liberties with folklore to suit my plot."[1]

Consequently, her story contains one of the most eclectic uses of magic you will ever read. It isn't always clear when the magic operates in the same manner as where it was borrowed from, or if it has been adapted and changed to fit the *Harry Potter* world. Sometimes the magic in *Harry Potter* mimics the traditional fairy tale, sometimes it borrows from ancient mythology, while at other times the magic is more like high-technology similar to what would be used in a science fiction story. Sometimes the magic is humorous and sometimes it is very serious. Sometimes the magic is purely

---

[1] *Harry Potter and Me,* BBC Christmas Special, December 28, 2001, http://www.accio-quote.org

mechanical, sometimes it involves ghosts and goblins, while at other times the magic involves the will power of the wizard. In one of the most dramatic scenes in the books, Voldemort conducts a blood ritual in order to restore his body to life. On top of all that, in the world of *Harry Potter*, the magic doesn't always work. A spell can go wrong, or a device can get damaged, and produce a result that is quite different from what the wizard intended.

The world of *Harry Potter* is also a blend of realism, adaptation and invention. A typical fairy tale takes place in a magical world that is completely separate from our world, or at least placed so far in the past or so far away that it has nothing to do with our world. For example, Tolkein's *The Lord of the Rings* takes place in a mythical place known only as Middle Earth, Le Guin's *Earthsea* is a completely invented world that is distinct from our own, while Lewis's *Chronicles of Narnia* takes place in parallel worlds. Rowling's invented world is unlike any of these. As Rowling stated in an interview, the world of *Harry Potter* is

> "like the real world in a very distorted mirror. We're not going off to a different planet, we're not going through timewarps. It is a fantastic world that has to live shoulder-by-shoulder with the real world."[2]

Her eclectic blend of fantasy and reality is like our own world with a magical element added to it. Often reviewers try to compare and contrast *Harry Potter* with *The Lord of the Rings* or *Chronicles of Narnia*, but a better comparison would be with the world of Gulliver in *Gulliver's Travels*. The world of *Harry Potter* is closer to a parody than a pure sub-creation typical of fantasy stories and that affects how we analyze and interpret the story. An interesting idea to consider is that the very form of the story is somehow a reflection of our world.

Children born since 1980 have never lived in a world without micro-computers. Children born since 1990 have never known a world without the Internet. The changes in our world that these two technologies have created are enormous. Knowledge today is

---

[2] *Harry Potter and Me*

becoming less and less tangible and more and more virtual such that computer simulation has reached the point where it is often difficult to tell what is "real" and what is not. If you can imagine something you can probably program it into a computer. You can take scanned images, manipulate them on the computer and produce an image that puts real things into a completely imagined context, and vice versa. You can program simulated devices that operate in a manner that violates all known laws of physics. Open a computer and you will not find any file folders, documents, or financial records. Yet we speak of those things as being on or in the computer. In other words, we increasingly live in a world that is a blend of virtual and physical, simulation and reality. We indeed live in a world where fantasy resides side-by-side with reality, just as in *Harry Potter*.

Current computer simulation is a continuation of a trend that started over a century ago with the invention of photography followed by the development of moving pictures. With the ability to capture an image and then process and reprint that image, it became possible to alter an image and yet make it appear real. Today we may consider early cinematic effects primitive, but even those early effects began to call into question what is real and what is fantasy. With reliance on radio then television and video for facts about the world we live in, our knowledge of what is real begins to depend more and more on trust that we are not being manipulated with invented images. In our world today it is increasingly difficult to state categorically that something is real as opposed to virtual.

To reiterate, and avoid any possible misunderstanding, what I am referring to is the form (and genre) of *Harry Potter*, not the content. What the literary *form* reflects is a world of magic and non-magic together. Rowling could have chosen to use realism as the form of the books and avoided any use of magic. Likewise, she could have written a straight fantasy story and removed any doubt that the elements of the story are invented. By blending the two forms, she has created a difficult problem for interpreters of the books. We cannot simply label every object or character in the books as real and proceed to interpret on that basis. Neither can we treat all the elements as fantasy and arbitrarily attach some allegorical meaning. This leaves interpreters arguing over which elements in the story should be considered real and which fantasy.

The only way we can honestly handle this situation is to be very careful when interpreting the themes in *Harry Potter*. We have to make sure that we don't get caught up in arguments that are based on trying to categorize the elements of the story as to which are real and which are invented. We can look at the magic in the story solely in terms of literary purpose without any problem. We can analyze the actions of the characters and see how they express moral ideals. We can even create analogies about the relationships of the actions of the characters to the elements of magic in the stories. But, because the line that divides the realism and the fantasy is vague, we must be very careful when claiming that any one object is inherently the same as something in our world.

Considering all of this together, *Harry Potter* presents an interesting reflection of the world we live in. It is a reflection of our world, not because the magic can somehow be compared to occult practice past or present, but rather because the eclectic blend of fantasy and realism is not all that different from the high-tech world we live in. Our world truly is a blend of fantasy and reality.

Magical Literary Devices

Harry Potter is a literary work and any one interpreting the magical elements must first see if the magic can be explained solely in literary terms. Looking at the magic in literary terms is important in understanding the overall story and how it works, while hopefully adding to the enjoyment of the books as well.

Unless a story takes place in one location, there must be a way for the characters to get from one place to another and also communicate with each other within the time limits of the story. If the characters need several weeks to get to a location, then the story cannot take place in less time and remain believable. This can present a problem for the author if subsequent events in different locations need to be closely spaced in time.

Since the wizards don't normally make use of Muggle technology, the author must provide them some other means of transportation and communication. One advantage of using magic in a story is that the author can move characters around quickly by unexplained magical means, shortening journeys that might not otherwise be possible within the time allotted to the characters and the events of the story. Rowling has borrowed, adapted and invented several forms of magic to allow the characters to communicate and move from place to place quickly and out of sight of the Muggles.

One form of transportation we encounter regularly in the story is the Hogwarts Express, a magical train that carries the students to and from school. Placing the students on a train recalls nostalgic images of a bygone era, but the Hogwarts Express is not simply an entertaining and unusual feature of the story. It serves several important literary purposes as well.

The hidden entry to platform 9-3/4 and the magical Hogwarts Express together provide a literary device that helps explain why the

Muggles cannot stumble upon Hogwarts. Since the world of *Harry Potter* is our world with magical elements blended in, the story cannot make sense unless the author provides an explanation of why the Muggles are not generally aware of the wizards. Some of the magic, such as the hidden train platform, serves this purpose.

The students' travel by train also allows time to setup the story that will unfold in the ensuing episode. The dialogue between the students during the ride to Hogwarts provides commentary, backstory information, and foreshadowing of the conflicts that will arise as the story progresses. Events that take place on the train serve a similar literary purpose. For example, the appearance of the Dementors, their attack on Harry and his rescue by Professor Lupin, provide an introduction to the events that follow in *Prisoner of Askaban*. We are left wondering why a professor was on the train, why are the dementors running loose and why did they single out Harry for attack? If the students were transported to Hogwarts by other means, the time for these events to take place might not be available to the author, or would have to be somehow worked in before or after arrival. Having them take place on the train is a clever and inventive double use of an element in the story.

It is also at the train station and on the train that Harry first encounters the other students that play an important role in the story. These encounters often serve to introduce new characters and establish their future relationships to Harry. Harry's encounter with Draco Malfoy sets the tone of their ongoing conflict, while Harry's encounter with Ron and Hermione creates a bond that will last throughout their school years together. Other means of travel are available to the wizards and are used later in the story. However, riding a train together gives the characters time to learn something about each other. The development of their relationships could not take place during the journey to Hogwarts if a quicker form of transportation was used.

The Portkey is another inventive and useful device for transportation of the characters. Unlike the Hogwarts Express, the Portkey allows nearly instantaneous travel. Initially we see it presented as a means of wizard travel that is somewhat limited and rarely used because it must be tightly regulated. Towards the end of *Goblet of Fire* the Portkey plays an important role in the story. By means of an unregulated Portkey disguised as the Triwizard tournament trophy, Harry and Cedric are suddenly transported to the graveyard where Voldemort waits. This isn't just a clever or arbitrary insertion into the story. Voldemort needs to get Harry alone, away from Hogwarts and the protection of Dumbledore, in order to use Harry as the means of his own revival. No other means of transportation, magical or otherwise, could easily serve this purpose. For example, if Harry were kidnapped or led to Voldemort by other means, there might be enough story time for other characters to locate him before he reaches Voldemort's location. The author would have to invent some reason why they did not do so. The instantaneous transportation of Harry prevents that from happening. We can see in retrospect that the introduction and explanation of the Portkey early in the episode is needed to set up this confrontation between Harry and Voldemort. We also are told why the Portkey is not the preferred means of travel to and from Hogwarts. It is in the form of an ordinary object and thus not easy for the characters to recognize. Altogether, the characteristics of the Portkey fit perfectly into the needs of the plot.

The ability of the characters to communicate at long distance is another aspect of storytelling that is related to transportation. The author needs a way for characters in different locations to send information back and forth. The contents of these communications help us understand the characters by conveying knowledge of events in their lives. The letters also provide information to Harry in his ongoing search for clues. As with transportation, the wizards don't use Muggle communication technology (they can't even understand how to use a telephone) and must be provided with some magically appropriate means instead. In *Harry Potter*, the characters use messenger Owls for this purpose. They can also use a fireplace, a mirror, or some other enchanted device to the same effect when the use of Owls would not make sense to the story.

The Hogwarts Express, the Night Bus, flying brooms, flying cars, Portkeys, the Floo Network, apparition, and messenger Owls all serve a similar literary purpose. All of these devices can best be seen as replacements for the technology of our world that serve a complementary purpose within the magical world of *Harry Potter*. They are inventive, entertaining, and useful literary devices that make the plot succeed.

In any mystery or detective story the hero must come to understand what events took place in the past that led up to and caused the current situation. We refer to such details as the backstory. Without this information the hero cannot solve the mystery and bring it to a conclusion. In the case of *Harry Potter,* many critical events took place long before Harry was born and this presents another literary problem for the storyteller. Typical literary devices used to present the backstory are flashback, interviews with eye witnesses, books, photographs, paintings and drawings, along with other forensic evidence collected from the scene where events took place. For some of the backstory Rowling uses these standard techniques. In a fantasy story that makes use of magic, the author can also invent one or more magical devices for this purpose instead. When thinking about the magical elements in the story, always remember that the reader usually only knows what Harry knows and until Harry receives the clue the reader is left "clueless" as well. Many of the magical devices are used to give Harry and us the clues.

One such device is the Pensieve, a magical basin that can hold an extracted memory. By diving into the basin, the wizards can become hidden observers of the memory, personally observing a replay of past events. The Pensieve (another pun by the way) plays a very important role in *The Half-Blood Prince.* Harry and Dumbledore repeatedly use the Pensieve to explore the history and motivation of Voldemort.

Harry's invisibility cloak and the Marauder's Map are used in a similar manner. By hiding under his cloak, Harry can secretly visit various places and listen in on conversations that provide him clues. Using the Marauder's Map, Harry can find passageways that allow him to move about in secret while searching for clues. These two devices allow Harry to be in places where he finds clues without the author having to invent some other reason for Harry to be there. Furthermore, because Harry receives the information directly, the author doesn't have to resort to a change of perspective in order to get these clues in front of the reader.

The ghosts that haunt Hogwarts are another source of information to fill in the backstory and provide clues to the hero. Because the ghosts have been around for many years, even centuries in some cases, the ghosts can become a source of historical information for Harry and his friends. Harry's interviews of the ghosts serve the same literary purpose as a detective's interviews of witnesses to past events. The ghosts provide a humorous element to the story as well, but in terms of the plot, they are critical as a source of historical information and facts. After the death of his godfather and friend Sirius Black, Harry goes to the ghost Nearly Headless Nick in order to understand death. Nick explains to Harry that ghosts are those whose souls have been separated from their bodies, but have not left the world. This, Nick goes on to explain, is different from those souls that have left the world. From this conversation we gain two vitally important facts about Harry's world. Ghosts are not spirits of the dead that have been brought back to life, but are the souls of those who became too attached to physical things and ended up trapped in an incorporeal form. Thus, the soul can be separated from the body but remain in the world. This explanation of the nature of the soul is important in understanding what Voldemort has done with the Horcruxes. Nick also explains that magic cannot bring back the dead, establishing an important limitation on magic in Harry's world. The wizards may be able to manipulate physical things, but they cannot create life where it does not exist. To do that would require a power greater than magic; the wizards are men, not gods. This fact is also important in understanding later events in the story.

Along with these magical means, Rowling employs the more typical eye witness interviews (such as those with Hagrid, Dumbledore and Sirius Black), and historical information from books in the library (usually supplied by Hermione). However, the magical literary devices add another level of entertainment and interest to the story. Rather than resort to the tried and true but clichéd methods of the "detective story", Rowling has both borrowed and invented to bring together different techniques of storytelling that create a varied, imaginative and fascinating literary solution.

Other magical devices fall into a miscellaneous category. One such device is the Deluminator. This device, invented by Albus Dumbledore, can capture light from any source that produces light, store the light inside the device, and then release the light back at a later point in time. We first encounter the Deluminator in the opening scene of *The Sorcerer's Stone* when Dumbledore uses it to turn out the street lamps on Privet Drive. With the lights out Hagrid can arrive on Sirius's enchanted motorcycle without being seen by the Muggles in the neighborhood. The Deluminator plays an important role in *The Deathly Hallows* when Harry and friends are imprisoned in a dark cellar underneath the Malfoy's house. One click of the Deluminator restores light and allows the characters to see who is who while they plan their escape.

Hermione's magic beaded bag is another interesting magical device that serves an important plot purpose. This apparently small bag can hold what seems to be an unlimited amount of stuff. But, because of its magical nature, it can be carried around without having to worry about the bulk or weight of whatever is inside. In *The Deathly Hallows* Hermione can carry all the supplies the three heroes need in their journey across the countryside without the characters having to explain why three teenagers are hauling around a wagonload of supplies. Whatever the author needs to put in the characters' hands can simply be drawn out of the bag, thus avoiding any story complications of how and where they could obtain just the precise items needed. Any time they need to acquire the objects by ordinary means, there is the possibility of discovery by Voldemort's agents. With Hermione's magic bag, most of what is needed is quickly and safely at hand. But when the author wants the characters to face danger of discovery or acquire additional clues, the items can be missing from the bag, requiring the characters to obtain them from a nearby village.

The preceding examples show how magic is used for plot purposes but there is another literary use of magic in *Harry Potter* as well. In the world of *Harry Potter*, sentient beings are divided between those who have magical ability and those who don't. Since the characters' magical ability is an innate ability, not something that can be learned by just anyone, magical ability divides people into classes. Throughout *Harry Potter* there is tension and conflict over which classes should be taught magic, who should be allowed to use it, who is to be treated as equals to wizards, and what relationships the various classes should have to each other. In other words, this difference results in questions of bigotry or prejudice. Establishing this limitation on magical ability lays the foundation for exploring the nature and effect of prejudice within a society. Thus, in addition to other literary purposes, the magic in *Harry Potter* is used to introduce moral themes.

These are just a few examples of how magic is used as a literary device in *Harry Potter*. Enumerating all of the literary uses of magic in the story would require many more pages of discussion. Hopefully, these few examples will serve as sufficient introduction of how magic in *Harry Potter* serves a purely literary purpose. Before we attach other meanings to the magical elements in the story, we should always look first to see if there is a literary purpose. Once we find out the literary purpose, we can much more easily interpret the magical elements in terms of what they might possibly mean symbolically, or discover that there is no need to find a symbolic meaning at all.

Magical Technology

As discussed in the previous essay, we can consider the magic in *Harry Potter* as nothing more than a complex of literary devices that solves plot problems while adding an imaginative and entertaining element to the story. However, even considering the magic as literary device, the question still remains of whether or not the magic in the world of *Harry Potter* can be used in an analogy with something in the real world other than the occult. After all, we do use the term "magic" to refer to things other than the occult.

When I was first reading *Harry Potter* I couldn't help thinking that the magical devices had a distinct similarity to the modern technology that I work with on a daily basis. To those who have never thought of technology this way, it may seem ludicrous to treat technology as something akin to magic. However, the science fiction writer Arthur C. Clarke is famous for his statement that "Any sufficiently advanced technology is indistinguishable from magic."[1] Larry Niven, another well-known writer of science fiction and fantasy, expressed this same idea conversely as "any sufficiently advanced magic is indistinguishable from technology."[2] This may seem like a strange idea at first, but consider the following.

Of all the people who use computers on a daily basis, how many can explain the operation of a microprocessor? The typical computer user knows that only certain keystrokes in the right combination will produce the desired effect but does not know why. Isn't that a kind of magic? Because we perceive the computer as technology and assume that somewhere there is somebody who invented this stuff and understands how it works, we think of it as mechanical and not

---

[1] , This is known as "Clarke's Third Law" and is from "Hazards of Prophecy: The Failure of Imagination", in *Profiles of the Future* (1962).
http://en.wikipedia.org/wiki/Clarke's_three_laws
[2] http://en.wikipedia.org/wiki/Niven's_Laws

magical. Yet, one definition of magic is "something that is inexplicable." For most people the internal operations of a computer are completely mysterious and therefore a kind of magic.

If I told you that every time you accessed a web site on the Internet you were spawning a demon to do magic would you believe me? Consider the following definitions from a dictionary of computer jargon known as *The Jargon File*.[3]

> **daemon**: /day-mn/, /dee-mn/, n.
> A program that is not invoked explicitly, but lies dormant waiting for some condition(s) to occur. The idea is that the perpetrator of the condition need not be aware that a daemon is lurking (though often a program will commit an action only because it knows that it will implicitly invoke a daemon). Daemon and demon are often used interchangeably, but seem to have distinct connotations.

> **spawn**: n. vi.
> In Unix parlance, to create a child process from within a process. Technically this is a 'fork'; the term 'spawn' is a bit more general and is used for threads (lightweight processes) as well as traditional heavyweight processes

> **magic**
> 1. adj. As yet unexplained, or too complicated to explain; ... 2. adj. Characteristic of something that works although no one really understands why (this is especially called black magic). 3. n. A feature not generally publicized that allows something otherwise impossible, or a feature formerly in that category but now unveiled. 4. n. The ultimate goal of all engineering & development, elegance in the extreme; from the first corollary to Clarke's Third

---

[3] http://www.catb.org/jargon. The Jargon File is also published in printed form as *The New Hacker's Dictionary* (MIT Press).

Law: "Any technology distinguishable from magic is insufficiently advanced".

Computer programmers love to borrow terms and adapt their meaning through analogies and metaphors. However, if we were to take these words in their ordinary sense, it would appear that the Internet is based on some occult, supernatural power! Of course, no one really believes that about computers, do they? We realize that this is a form of tongue-in-cheek humor and don't consider a computer as something supernatural. The meaning of a word can be extended by adapting it into a new context with a new usage, and that is what programmers have done. Authors of fiction often do the same thing with words.

In a fantasy novel, and to some extent in any work of fiction, the author does not need to explain how things in the story really work. The author can take real places and move them around and alter them, within limits. Likewise the author can add or remove capabilities from some object that we know very well. For example, computers in fictional stories often have capabilities that far exceed those of real life or work differently than our desktop computers. We usually call these types of adaptations "literary license" or something equivalent. Thus, there is a limitation in how far we need to go in making an explanation of how the magic in *Harry Potter* actually works or drawing comparisons to things in our world. As long as the magic is believable in the context of the story we don't have to make any explanation at all. However, there is an interesting parallel between the magic in *Harry Potter* and today's highly advanced technology. First, we need to see if we can legitimately compare the story's magic to technology.

From the *Harry Potter* books we find out that the only real difference between Muggles and wizards is that the wizards have an innate ability to do magic. Most wizards are born to wizard parents, but some like Hermione Granger are the children of Muggles. Furthermore, not all wizard children have the ability to do magic and are called Squibs. Filch, the caretaker of Hogwarts, is one example. In one scene from *The Chamber of Secrets*, we learn that Filch has ordered *Kwikspell*, a self-help book on magic, in an effort to learn magic. However, it won't do him any good. This is important, since it indicates that magic in *Harry Potter* is not something that everyone can learn how to do. It is an ability that you must be born with. That seems to make magic different from technology.

However, if we are to make an analogy between *Harry Potter* and the real world, we can treat magical ability as something akin to abilities caused by a genetic variation. For example, we could think of it as something like color blindness. Imagine if some device could only be used by people who could discriminate between red and green. Those who are color blind would never be able to use the device, or could only make limited use of it. To extend the comparison a little further, imagine there was a technology that required the ability to hear sounds above 20,000 Hz. That is the normal upper limit of human hearing, so this technology would require something like a genetic mutation that produced a greater hearing ability in some people. Only those people with this extraordinary hearing ability would be able to use the technology. We might even imagine that these "super-frequency" types would keep this ability a secret in order to avoid being considered freaks or to create some advantage over others lacking the ability. That is a fair analogy of magical ability in *Harry Potter* that doesn't preclude treating the magic similarly to technology.

When you look at how magical devices in *Harry Potter* are used, developed and improved, there is an even closer analogy with technology. In *Quidditch Through The Ages*, there is a lengthy discussion of the development of the flying broom. It reads much like a history of a scientific discovery followed by subsequent application and improvement as technology.

In *The Half-blood Prince* Harry obtains a potions book that has many marginal notes showing alternative methods of producing potions. Potions seem to work in a manner much like advanced chemistry.

The magic wand the wizards use is another example. The wand is not simply a piece of wood but must have something with magical properties embedded into it before it can be used for magic. As Harry eventually finds out through a conversation with Ollivander, there is much about the wizard's magic wand that even the wizard's don't fully understand. That's likewise true of much of our modern technology. For example, scientists still do not have a complete understanding of electricity, even though we use it extensively in our day to day lives. We often have to put a bit of "magic" called a battery into our devices before they do anything useful.

When a wizard in *Harry Potter* has his wand knocked away, his ability to cast or block spells is eliminated, or at least greatly reduced. Likewise, if the wand is not pointed in the right direction the spell will not affect the object the wizard wants to affect. Consider this passage from near the end of *The Half-blood Prince.*

> Harry tore past Hagrid and his opponent, took aim at Snape's back, and yelled, *"Stupefy!"*
>
> He missed; the jet of red light soared past Snape's head; ... Twenty yards apart, he and Harry looked at each other before raising their wands simultaneously.
>
> *"Cruc—"*
>
> But Snape parried the curse, knocking Harry backward off his feet before he could complete it;...
>
> *"Incarc—"* Harry roared, but Snape deflected the spell with an almost lazy flick of his arm.

The wand waving and hurling of spells between Harry and Snape continues until Snape knocks the wand out of Harry's hand. The magic wand in this scene is similar to a real world sword or gun, or perhaps an "energy beam" weapon from a science fiction story, but with a bit of artificial intelligence built in.

We also learn that spells and charms can be both invented and improved. Returning to the computer analogy for an example, it is much like what a computer programmer does. The computer only responds to the right words (it's instruction set), which act much like an incantation. However, the programmer can rearrange and combine keywords to invent new "spells" and make the computer do something it had not done before. We call these new "incantations" computer programs. If the computer is operated by a voice recognition system, the analogy is even closer. Of course the analogy is not perfect, but the two ideas are very similar.

Some may still object that the magic wand amplifies the thoughts and will of the wizard and thus is nothing like a computer. However, those of us who work with computers will tell you that it is exactly like a computer. You see, we don't really need computers. As has been said, and every programmer knows, if we could run our software just as fast without them, we would throw the computers away as an unnecessary nuisance. In fact, we often speak of a computer as a "thought amplifier" because it does the same calculations and data retrieval that we normally could do in our brain, just much faster and with more consistency.

Another similarity exists between divination and Arithmancy in *Harry Potter* and statistics and trend prediction in our world. Every day people open up their newspapers and engage in a form of divination. I'm not referring to the Astrology pages, but to the business news section. The business section is filled with tables and charts of stock prices and market trends. Those who invest will spend time with pages of charts trying to see a pattern in the shape of the graphs. It's not that much different from trying to predict the future by gazing into a crystal ball or reading the dregs from a cup of tea. Both activities seem to have about the same level of accuracy as well.

Based on what is described in the story, the idea that the magic in *Harry Potter* is analogous to technology is a good fit and a fair and workable interpretation. No single interpretation of the magic will fit all examples in the story exactly, nor does it have to. However, the comparison of most magic in *Harry Potter* to technology is very close whether or not Rowling intended it that way.[4] Although not a perfect analogy, the similarity between magic and technology is close enough that we can interpret it as such and then draw some interesting comparisons between life in the world of *Harry Potter* and life in our world. We can state the analogy as: magic is to wizards as technology is to Muggles.

---

[4] Both magic and science can be seen as attempts to control natural forces and there are various historians that link the development of modern science to magic of the late renaissance (e.g. Lynn Thorndike). The thesis is based on treating magic as a mechanical and mathematical system that models and describes manipulation of natural phenomena. It is possible that Rowling used information from these books in developing the magic for Harry Potter, but I have not been able to confirm this. In an interview for amazon.com in 1999, Rowling did state, "We owe a lot of our scientific knowledge to the alchemists."

An interesting thing that I noticed while reading the *Harry Potter* books is that life for the wizards is not all that different from life for the Muggles in many aspects. Both have to go to school to develop their natural skills, choose a career based on abilities and desires, and then go to work and earn money to buy things they need. Both are born and both die. What's more, the wizards have laws that regulate the use of magic, regulate affairs between wizards, and regulate relationships between Muggles and wizards. This requires a political institution, the Ministry of Magic, with all the typical political intrigue, bureaucratic interference, and bumbling that comes with it. Because they have laws to enforce, the wizards have policemen in the form of Aurors and have a prison with guards to hold and punish law breakers. Even the wizard's newspapers don't seem to be any different. They often print innuendo, rumor and slander instead of objective fact and sometimes end up acting as a propaganda facility for the government. Apart from the use of magic as opposed to scientific technology, and some differences in dress and appearance, there really is not that much difference between the wizards and the Muggles. Consequently, one could conclude there is not all that much advantage to being a wizard. Much like a natural athletic ability, it would be nice, but a person's life will go on pretty much the same with or without it.

Another aspect of magic in *Harry Potter* is that the magic is not omnipotent but is actually limited in many ways. Magic can heal, with the right herbs, potions and spells, but cannot bring someone who has died back to life. In some cases the magic cannot counter curses either, as in the case of Neville Longbottom's parents or Dumbledore's hand. We also find out that the food the wizards eat is not created by magic, even if it is prepared and served by magic. Magic potions can take months to prepare and require specific magical ingredients that have to be collected or purchased and wands require rare elements to make as well. The wizards aren't able to conjure up everything *ex nihilo*. Wizards can fall off their brooms and get hurt, and apparating can produce some really uncomfortable and potentially dangerous side effects. In short, the magic is useful but doesn't provide all of a wizard's needs in life. That sounds a lot like technology.

Also, we don't consider people good or bad simply because they use some particular technology. That is exactly how things are portrayed in *Harry Potter*. What makes Voldemort and the Death Eaters evil is not simply that they use magic. The opponents of Voldemort also use magic, although there are limits they will place on themselves that Voldemort will not. Voldemort and his followers will use the "unforgivable curses" representing torture, enslavement and murder without hesitation. The good guys won't except under exceptional circumstances such as self-defense.

For the most part we do not talk about a battle between "white technology" and "black technology" although there are some areas where perhaps we should. Just as there are unforgivable curses in the wizard world, there are unforgivable uses of technology in ours. Nuclear bombs, biological weapons, some applications of genetic engineering, and synthesized hallucinogenic drugs are some examples of things that probably should have been left alone.

Perhaps even more important is the fact that Harry does not truly overcome Voldemort's attacks through equivalent use of magic. Harry is no match for Voldemort in either knowledge or experience of spells, hexes and charms, yet at each trial Harry succeeds. If you think about it you will see that Harry overcomes evil with something other than the same magic being used against him. He may use some of the same magical devices and spells along the way, but in the end it is the character, virtue and moral choices of Harry and others that win the battle. Lily's sacrificial love for her son protects him from Quirrell. Harry's courage and fidelity in the Chamber of Secrets allows him to pull the sword out of the hat. His compassion, mercy and self-sacrifice are vital factors in other battles. In the end, Harry overcomes evil with good, the highest "magic" of all.

Consider the magic of *Harry Potter* as technology and think of what that implies for us. I think this leads us to consider an important fact of human life. As Dumbledore explains to Harry at the end of *The Sorcerer's Stone:*

> "You know, the Stone was really not such a wonderful thing. As much money and life as you could want! The two things most human beings would choose above all—the trouble is, humans do have a knack of choosing precisely those things that are worst for them."

No matter how powerful our technology becomes, even if it were to be so advanced that it could provide for all our material desires, we would still have to contend with the same problems of human nature and good and evil. We would still have to make moral choices and accept the consequences of our choices when we choose wrongly. Another writer on *Harry Potter* came to a similar conclusion. In his essay, *Harry Potter's Magic,* Wheaton College Professor Alan Jacobs wrote:

> Christians are perhaps right to be wary of an overly positive portrayal of magic, but the Harry Potter books don't do that: in them magic is often fun, often surprising and exciting, but also always potentially dangerous.
>
> And so, it should be said, is the technology that has resulted from the victory of experimental science. Perhaps the most important question I could ask my Christian friends who mistrust the Harry Potter books is this: is your concern about the portrayal of this imaginary magical technology matched by a concern for the effects of the technology that in our world displaced magic? The technocrats of this world hold in their hands powers almost infinitely greater than those of Albus Dumbledore and Voldemort: how worried are we about them, and their influence over our children? Not worried enough, I would say.[5]

I couldn't agree more. Hoping for a solution to the problems of life through magic is no worse than betting all of our future on technology. Neither one will ultimately work to solve all our problems. We must find purpose in life by pursuing virtue, not mere technology. And, like Harry, we must overcome evil with good.

---

[5] Alan Jacobs, "Harry Potter's Magic," *First Things* 99 (January 2000): 35-38, http://www.firstthings.com/

Law, Morality and Necessity

Moral issues are rarely simple, despite our desire for them to be so. In most instances we are faced with a complex moral situation where there may not be a clear-cut choice between good and evil or right and wrong. This may appear to some to be moral ambiguity and relativism, but is more accurately described as moral complexity. In an essay titled *Magic, Muggles, and Moral Imagination,* philosophy professor David Bagget explains:

> Moral complexities don't entail that everything ethical is colored gray and up for grabs. That a character like Harry may have flaws doesn't mean he's not a hero or virtuous. That a rule (such as a prohibition against lying) may admit of exceptions doesn't mean it ought not be followed. That moral dilemmas may require us to choose the lesser of two evils doesn't mean that there's no moral difference between them.[1]

An example of moral complexity shows up in the first *Harry Potter* book during the flying broom lesson. In this scene Harry deliberately ignores the teacher's instruction for the children to not get on their flying brooms while she is away. Yet, despite ignoring the teacher's instructions, Harry is rewarded with a place on the Quidditch team. This seems strange to Hermione. As she stomps up the stairs behind Harry, she says, "So I suppose you think that's a reward for breaking rules?" But Hermione's attitude is based on a misunderstanding.

---

[1] David Bagget, *Magic, Muggles, and Moral Imagination,* published in *Harry Potter and Philosophy* (Open Court publishing, 2004), p. 165.

   In this scene, Madame Hooch must take a student to the infirmary and tells the other students to stay on the ground and off their flying brooms while she is away or else risk expulsion. That's a typical and very reasonable behavior for a good teacher. She is trying to protect the students from harm by restricting their actions and ignoring that restriction should be punished, one would think. Draco Malfoy ignores the teacher's restrictions and takes advantage of her absence to cause grief for another student, Neville Longbottom. Neville is a shy, often weak, forgetful boy who has been sent a Remembrall by his Grandmother. In an earlier scene Draco tries to get the Remembrall from Neville. Now, with Neville off to the infirmary, Draco grabs the device and flies off with it. Harry's eventual response is to jump on his broom and go after Draco. In the end, Harry retrieves the Remembrall by diving towards the ground, catching the ball just before it hits the ground. Harry's rescue of the Remembrall is seen by Professor McGonagall and it is at that point that she takes Harry to the captain of the Quidditch team and has him put on the team.

   Before trying to find some moral lesson in this scene, we should start by looking at it from a literary perspective. Many important scenes that follow take place on the Quidditch pitch and the author has to get Harry onto the Quidditch team. However, Harry has never even seen a Quidditch match, much less played the game. First year students at Hogwarts are not allowed to even try out for the team. The flying lesson scene serves the important function of solving this sticky plot problem. First, it takes place before the Quidditch team tryouts, and provides a plausible explanation why Harry does not replace an existing player. Furthermore, if the teachers were around, Harry would not be able to zoom around on his broom discovering and demonstrating his instinctive, natural ability. Thus, one important purpose of this scene is to move the plot forward. As Harry remarks to Ron, "If [Draco] hadn't stolen Neville's Remembrall I wouldn't be on the team...." Moreover, the actions of Harry when the teacher is away are typical of how he will act throughout the story. Thus, in addition to placing Harry on the Quidditch team, the flying lesson scene establishes important character traits for both Harry and Draco. Harry's blood boils at the idea of the injustice done by Draco and he instinctively reacts as a hero. This is one of the first scenes where we see Harry courageously responding to injustice and evil. We also see that Draco is effectively a coward. This contrast between courage and cowardice plays out over the course of the books.

Looking at all the elements of the scene we see that Harry was not rewarded because he broke the rules, as Hermione thought. Harry was put on the team because he demonstrated a natural ability that would make him a good Quidditch player. That ability would have been discovered in any case and is in no way a reward for misbehaving. We also find out that McGonagall is tired of Gryffindor always losing to Slytherin and her action of ignoring the infraction is better understood as motivated by that alone. In any case, the reward is coincidental, not an intended or planned consequence of misbehaving.

Nevertheless, Harry was not punished for violating the teacher's orders and that seems to make breaking the rules a good thing. However, we should consider that many of the situations in the books like the one just described involve rules and regulations established for a specific situation, not universal or natural laws. These types of temporary rules cannot be put on the same level of importance as absolute moral principles. In other words, they are "traditions of men" not "carved in stone by the hand of God." We sometimes can come to believe that any infraction of rules is wrong simply because it goes against authority. The fallacy in thinking that way should be obvious.

The real reason Harry often goes unpunished is simply because those responsible for upholding the rules are the same ones who made the rules in the first place. As such, they have the authority to suspend or change the rules when they realize that enforcement would lead to additional harm and not justice. As Dumbledore remarks at the end of *Chamber of Secrets:*

> "I seem to remember telling you both that I would have to expel you if you broke any more school rules," said Dumbledore.
>
> Ron opened his mouth in horror.
>
> "Which goes to show that the best of us must sometimes eat our words," Dumbledore went on, smiling.

As Dumbledore realizes, the rules had to be broken in order to achieve a just resolution. That does leave us with the question of when it is valid to change or suspend the rules. If disregard for law is arbitrarily ignored, then law loses its effectiveness.

Going back to the flying lesson scene, we need to look more closely at the situation that motivated Harry's choice. The scene could have been written such that Harry took advantage of the teacher's absence to do what he wanted. That would express a self-serving disregard and disdain for authority. But it is not Harry who demonstrates that disdain; Draco is the one who has no respect for the teacher's authority. Draco's action changed the situation from what it was when Madame Hooch walked away. No longer is it simply a group of students standing around waiting for the teacher to return. Harry's behavior is not motivated by a disdain for rules or any other self-serving desire, but by a desire to defend someone who is under attack. An injustice has been done, there is no one else there to stop it, and in that situation Harry's instinct takes over. Harry is responding as a hero, a defender of another who cannot defend himself. That's a choice of action that most of us would consider morally correct and is entirely within character for Harry. His action may have been impertinent and imprudent, typical of adolescents, but it is not immoral behavior. If we want to consider Harry's receipt of his own flying broom and placement on the Quidditch team as a reward for his actions, we should see it symbolically as a reward that results from fighting against injustice. Whenever we pursue justice for others, in other words, we gain an unexpected reward for ourselves.

Although trivial on the surface, the flying lesson scene is typical of the moral questions that we encounter in life. How do you respond to a schoolyard bully when the teacher is not available? We must evaluate two actions, each of which might cause harm, and choose the better of the two. We have to ask, as Hamlet did, "Whether 'tis nobler in the mind to suffer/The slings and arrows of outrageous fortune/Or to take arms against a sea of troubles/And by opposing end them."

An analogy to a simpler, yet common situation might help to make this principle clear. Is it allowable for an ambulance to ignore the traffic regulations? A simple answer of "yes" does not really explain the situation, and we need to stop and think more deeply about the question. The correct answer is, "It depends on the situation." Unless an ambulance is going to or from the scene of an emergency, the ambulance driver has no more right to violate the traffic regulations than any other driver on the road. It is only when the ambulance is responding to an emergency that it may turn on a flashing light and loud siren, exceed the speed limit and ignore traffic control signals. It is the emergency situation that creates the need to suspend the normal traffic regulations.

It is naïve to think of this in purely utilitarian terms. While it is true that the normal regulations are ignored by the ambulance, the reason for setting aside the regulations is not simply for the sake of convenience. To understand this concept we have to think of the purpose and intent of the traffic regulations. We regulate traffic in order to preserve the peace and public safety. For that reason, a violation of the traffic regulations is a potential threat to other members of the community. However, in the case of an emergency, the life of someone is at stake. If the purpose of the law is to preserve life, then the law must allow a special case for emergency situations. Although the speeding ambulance may appear to be discarding the law, it is in fact upholding the intent and purpose of the law, namely, to preserve the well being of members of the community.

Of course, there is a significant difference between an ambulance speeding to the scene of an accident and handling a schoolyard bully. But in both cases we have to look at all aspects of a situation in order to evaluate the morality of an action. This is a subtle, but important, distinction between utilitarian morals, moral relativism, and moral complexity. Moral behavior cannot be reduced down to simply following the rules, but must take into account all aspects of the situation and weigh each action in light of some overriding moral principle.

Valid law always seeks to achieve the higher purpose of justice. As it is sometimes said, the intent of the law is the force of the law. If following the letter of the law is in conflict with the intent of the law, then actions must be chosen to reach that intent, even if the actions go against the letter of the law. To some this may appear to be saying that the end justifies the means. However, the correct understanding is that the means and the end must be unified in intent. A lawful means that produces an unjust end is no more valid than an unlawful means that reaches a just end. For this reason, well written laws allow for exigent circumstances, emergency, and necessity. If the law does not allow for these situations, then the law must be reevaluated when these conditions are present.

As discussed previously, a literary work can be used to reflect conditions in our real world society. Most of us live within societies run by both public and private bureaucracies where we are wrapped up in miles of red tape and buried under reams of regulations. At times the bureaucratic rule-making becomes so intrusive that the only way to get anything done is to ignore the rules, or at least find some way to get around them. The characters in *Harry Potter* face the same problem in the person of Delores Umbridge.

Umbridge is one of those bureaucrats that never met a difficult situation that she couldn't further mess up by writing a new regulation. Her intervention at Hogwarts as the Defense Against the Dark Arts teacher turns into a disaster for the students. At the time they most need instruction, she turns the class into a farce. Any complaints or hint of rebellion is dealt with harshly. After all, rules are rules and those who break the rules must be punished. As Umbridge gains more and more influence, usurping power by arbitrary regulation, the students are forced to find a solution outside the normal procedures, eventually establishing Dumbledore's Army.

We could look at the actions of the students in a superficial manner and accuse them of having a disdain for authority and a rebellious attitude toward rules, but the events of the story make that conclusion absurd. The conflict the students and eventually the whole of wizard society had to reconcile was the abuse of authority by bureaucrats. Under those conditions, the only appropriate and heroic thing to do is to blatantly ignore the rules. Rowling's sarcastic depiction of the heavy hand of bureaucracy and the student's response is an excellent depiction of the conditions we face in our world and what we often have to do in response. Under normal conditions we follow the rules so that we may live within a peaceful society. But there are times when that attitude simply won't work.

There is an even more direct expression of this concept in *Harry Potter and the Order of the Phoenix*. At the beginning of this episode Harry and his cousin are attacked by Dementors. Harry responds by producing his *Patronus* charm, succeeds in driving the Dementors away, and thus rescues himself and his cousin. This action violates two of the laws for the wizard community. Harry is an underage wizard and restricted in the use of magic outside of school. In addition, wizards are prohibited from performing magic in the presence of Muggles. Harry has violated both of these laws in one act.

Harry is subsequently summoned to appear before the judges of the Wizengamot. The sudden change of time for appearance gives us a clue that maybe this tribunal is not wholly on the up and up, but more likely a setup by Harry's opponents. We find out later in the story that this is exactly the case. Fortunately for Harry, Dumbledore arrives in time to act as counsel. Before being rudely cut off by Fudge, Dumbledore reminds the Wizengamot that, "Clause seven of the Decree sates that magic may be used before Muggles in exceptional circumstances, and as those exceptional circumstances include situations that threaten the life of the wizard or witch himself..." Dumbledore correctly points out that the law includes provisions for use of magic by underage wizards when there is an emergency or necessity. A majority of the judges admit the truth of this provision of the law and Harry is not punished for his infraction.

The same analysis applies to moral behavior. Both the action and the consequence must be judged on the basis of a moral principle. When faced with moral dilemma, we choose the course of action that appears to best serve the greater moral principle, even if in doing so we introduce the possibility of some lesser harm. This is distinct from moral relativism. Moral relativism denies moral absolutes, replacing them with subjective values, and thus the moral principle changes when the person's desires change or the situation changes. In contrast, absolute moral principles remain in effect in all situations, but the action taken in each situation is the action appropriate to the moral principle. It's a subtle, but important distinction and one that is easy to miss.

Suspending the rules to allow for emergencies is an important and valid principle of law, but is also potentially dangerous. A misuse of the appeal to necessity is the typical response of an immoral person. Having done something wrong, and not wanting to suffer the consequences, an immoral person will usually create some kind of an excuse in the form of "it was necessary." Distinguishing between a valid appeal to necessity and an invalid one can be difficult at times. Yet it is something we must learn to do.

One sure way to test if an action was truly necessary is to see if the action is purely self-serving. There is a very clear example of this misapplication in *The Deathly Hallows*. Near the end of the book, Voldemort kills Snape solely for the purpose of gaining additional power for himself. Snape was not at that time threatening Voldemort, and was in fact considered Voldemort's chief ally. Yet, it served Voldemort's lust for power and that became the excuse that Voldemort gave to Snape as he killed him.

> "The Elder Wand belongs to the wizard who killed its last owner. You killed Albus Dumbledore. While you live, Severus, the Elder Wand cannot be truly mine."
> "My Lord!" Snape protested, raising his wand.
> "It cannot be any other way," said Voldemort.

Voldemort's actions from beginning to end are purely self-serving. For Voldemort, there is no law or rule other than to serve self-interest and he will readily violate any agreement or confidence if it serves his desire for more power. He accurately represents the nihilist who lives by the motto that the end justifies the means. By comparison, a valid use of the principle of necessity will seek the end of justice. This is a vitally important distinction and in *Harry Potter* the distinction is set out clearly throughout the books. Harry and his friends go unpunished for their infractions when to do so would clearly lead to injustice. Although there are times when the immature Harry steps over the line and does not get punished, he is usually left with a sense of remorse. Voldemort knows no remorse, and it is clearly the evil Voldemort whose actions exemplify immorality, not Harry. And that is exactly the way a good story should express moral principles.

These scenes, like many similar scenes in the books, present an excellent starting point for discussing the relationship of authority, law, morality, and necessity. The situations we encounter in life are often complex and a simplistic, legalistic understanding of morality will not adequately address the situation. If we try to think of moral behavior as a list of rules to follow, we hide this complexity and fail to grasp a true understanding of morality.

Sneaking Around

There is a lot of sneaking around in *Harry Potter*. Again and again, Harry and his friends sneak out of their rooms in violation of the regulations of Hogwarts. As Dumbledore says, they seem to have a certain "disdain for the rules." But all of this sneaking around serves an important plot purpose. Since Harry is the detective who must solve the riddle, he is the one who needs to discover the important clues. Sometimes the information obtained by sneaking around turns out to be incorrect and helps setup plot twists, but for the most part these scenes provide important clues to Harry and the reader. By comparison, this is much like a stakeout by a detective in a traditional mystery novel. It says nothing about whether or not you should spy on someone to get information; it is simply used as an effective way to get the information in front of the reader. In short, Harry and friends have to sneak around in order for the story to be told. Although there are other literary devices that could have been used, all that sneaking around is much more exciting to read. The threat of getting caught adds suspense to the story.

When Harry and his friends sneak around and violate the rules of Hogwarts, they are almost always doing so with the intent of gaining knowledge needed to defeat evil. The rules that disallow the students from leaving their rooms, or going into restricted sections of the library and the Forbidden Forest, are all intended to protect the students from harm. However, Harry's situation is unique. He is the focus of Voldemort's attack and his life is at risk. Simply staying in his room will not prevent harm to himself or the other students. In order to combat the evil that he faces, Harry must obtain information about the danger that he faces. Because that information is not available to him by other means, he has to sneak around to get the needed information. Furthermore, because Harry is at Hogwarts, the danger to Harry puts the other students at risk as well. His violations of the rules are motivated by, and ultimately lead to, protection of himself and the other students, not to their harm.

All this sneaking around, as with many of Harry's activities, is necessitated by a lack of knowledge. In some cases the information he needs is known by the adults, but is held back from Harry in some manner. Because of his need to obtain that knowledge, Harry is acting in a way that is dangerous to himself. This is a true moral dilemma where either course of action creates risk. In the end, the greater risk of ignorance outweighs the risk of wandering around out in the open.

This is another interesting and important aspect of moral choice. We often act on the basis of limited knowledge and because of our ignorance may make the wrong choice. To avoid making the wrong choice based on ignorance, we may have to bend the rules to obtain the knowledge we need. That doesn't always excuse our actions, but it is precisely the type of moral issue that we face in life. *Harry Potter* contains many good examples of what can go wrong when we don't have all the information we need and also what can go wrong if we are not careful in how we obtain that knowledge.

Along the same lines, Harry's lack of knowledge is due to the intentional withholding of that knowledge by Dumbledore and other adults. Dumbledore is motivated by a desire to protect Harry from things that Harry is not mature enough to face. Yet, as Dumbledore eventually admits, that decision on his part created a problem. As Dumbledore explains at the end of *The Order of the Phoenix:*

> "I cared about you too much," said Dumbledore simply. "I cared more for your happiness than your knowing the truth, more for your peace of mind than my plan, more for your life than the lives that might be lost if the plan failed. In other words, I acted exactly as Voledmort expects we fools who love to act.
>
> "Is there a defense? I defy anyone who has watched you as I have – and I have watched you more closely than you can have imagined – not to want to save you more pain that you had already suffered…"

"...And now, tonight, I know you have long been ready for the knowledge I have kept from you for so long, because you have proved that I should have placed the burden upon you before this. My only defense is this: I have watched you struggling under more burdens than any student who has ever passed through this school, and I could not bring myself to add another – the greatest one of all."

Had Dumbledore given Harry all of the information that was available, Harry might have avoided some of the bad choices he made. In addition, Harry might have been more likely to follow Dumbledore's advice. The Occulmancy lessons from Snape that Harry is given are a prime example. Harry's misplaced disdain for Snape and his lack of understanding of the connection with Voldemort prevent Harry from taking the lessons to completion. Had Dumbledore explained the reasons, Harry would have been more likely to gain the experience that he needed. Likewise, had Harry been told what was going on, he could possibly have avoided the trap set by Voldemort that led to the death of Sirius Black.

Out of love and concern for Harry, Dumbledore had decided to try to spare Harry the unpleasantness and burden of the truths that must at some time be known by him. This is always a difficult decision to make. When and how do we reveal truths to someone that they need to know but may not yet be prepared to accept? This is a good point that both children and adults need to understand. Children will need to trust the knowledge of adults even if they do not fully understand it. Likewise, adults need to be wary of being so overprotective of children that they do not prepare the children with the knowledge they need to accurately choose the proper action when faced with a moral choice. This difficult decision applies to all personal relationships as well, not just those between parents and children.

There is another subtle, but vitally important aspect of the search for knowledge that we must come to understand. As Dumbledore knows and explains to Harry, before we can reveal truths that are difficult to bear, a person must reach a point of maturity capable of accepting those truths. This is not simply because the person may not be able to emotionally bear up. Some information, if not wisely used, can be dangerous to the person who knows it. In other cases, the information may be something of value that we cannot risk revealing except to those we trust. Until a person has shown maturity, wisdom, and fidelity to the truth, we are not doing that person or ourselves any favor by revealing the truth to them. That is the conflict that Dumbledore has to deal with in regard to Harry. It is also the conflict that Harry and his companions face. They often do not reveal the truth of their actions when to do so would be misunderstood or misused by the recipient. It would be preferable, of course, if we could always speak the unvarnished truth, but the limits of human nature often prevent us from doing so.

The only way we can be sure the person can receive the knowledge we want to give them is to first allow them to act on their own, preferably in a limited and controlled situation. That way, we can see if they will develop the mature moral character worthy of our trust. As Dumbledore explains to Snape, "We have protected him because it has been essential to teach him, to raise him, to let him try his strength." Although Dumbledore has explained this to Harry in a roundabout way, it is only near the end of *Deathly Hallows* that Harry finally comes to understand. Harry had to go through a trial first to see if he was one worthy to bear the burden. Dumbledore may have been manipulating Harry, but it had to be done the way it was done. As Harry realizes, "Dumbledore had known that Harry would not duck out...because he had taken trouble to get to know him."

It is necessary to seek the truth in order to receive it. If we are not seeking the truth, anyone trying to give it to us will be ignored. Furthermore, it is in seeking the truth out of a love of the truth that we develop the moral character necessary for those who hold great truths. Harry is an archetypical seeker of the truth. His position on the Quidditch team portrays this symbolically, and we see it in his actions from the beginning to the end of the story.

By contrast, a failure to seek the truth is one of Voldemort's failings and contributes to his downfall. He seeks knowledge only for the purpose of power over others and to avoid death for himself. He will not investigate or attempt to understand things that do not give him power over others and in so doing he regularly discounts or ignores significant facts. In other words, unlike Harry, Voldemort does not seek truth for its own sake or for the sake of others. As

Dumbledore explained to Harry, "That which Voldemort does not value, he takes no trouble to comprehend."

Voldemort's attack on Harry as a baby is but one example. Voldemort could have waited to see how the boy would develop and then plan accordingly. He also could have waited to try and verify the prophecy, in which case he might have understood that only the boy that Voldemort marks is the one that will be a danger to him. But in his arrogance he decides to act immediately. Ironically, it was Voldemort's own choice, and his own arrogant and impatient action, that created the means of his downfall.

Even at the very end, when Harry tries to warn Voldemort and give him the knowledge he needs, Voldemort will not hear it:

> "I know things you don't know, Tom Riddle. I know lots of important things that you don't. Want to hear some, before you make another big mistake?"

But Voldemort has traveled too far and too long down a path of self-deception to hear the truth from anyone. He disdainfully assumes that the actions of others, like his own, could have had no other purpose than power and self aggrandizement. He has never sought the truth and cannot comprehend that others have. In so doing, he rejects the truth that Harry has learned. As Harry tells him, "You still don't get it, Riddle, do you? Possessing the wand isn't enough."

No, as Harry has come to learn, just as Dumbledore had to learn, possessing a thing, or knowing a thing, is not enough. Voldemort's power as a wizard may far exceed that of Harry, but Voldemort has never sought knowledge for the right reason and is left vulnerable because of that. He does not truly understand the nature of either the power he holds or the power used against him. He cannot understand how there could be a power greater than magic, and that those he despises have that power when he does not.

How and why we go about gaining knowledge is part of the quest for knowledge. First we must reach the point of maturity where we can accept difficult truths, and we must be tested to see if we are worthy. Furthermore, our intent in gaining knowledge and the purpose we seek to fulfill ultimately determines what truths we will discover. Those who seek knowledge for the proper purpose may have to search diligently and face danger to get it, but will ultimately gain what they desire and will have developed the moral character to know what to do with it as well.

Pride and Prejudice

Of all the many themes in *Harry Potter* there is one theme that stands out directly, with no equivocation at all, and runs as a constant from beginning to end of the story. The world of *Harry Potter* is filled with prejudice on all sides. Out of prejudice a variety of evils emerge.

We encounter prejudice from the very first chapter of the first book. Petunia Dursley, Harry Potter's aunt, has not spoken to the Potters in years "because her sister and her good-for-nothing husband were as unDursleyish as it was possible to be." It wasn't just James and Lily Potter either: "they didn't want Dudley mixing with a child like that." We quickly find out that the Dursleys don't mix with the Potters because the Potters are wizards and the Dursleys are not. When the baby Harry is left with the Dursleys, that prejudice spills over onto Harry and leads to a miserable childhood for a boy who has done nothing to deserve such treatment.

We usually think of prejudice of that type to be an irrational attitude based on nothing more than superficial and insignificant differences. But the source of Petunia's prejudice, as in most prejudice, runs deeper than that. We discover that source after Harry receives his letter from Hogwarts and is told his mother was a witch. When Harry asks about his mother, Petunia declares:

> "Oh, I was the only one who saw her for what
> she was – a freak! But for my mother and father, oh
> no, it was Lily this and Lily that, they were proud of
> having a witch in the family!"

In *The Deathly Hallows*, we find out that Petunia's anger is not simply that Lily was a witch and therefore adored by her parents, a simple case of sibling rivalry. When Lily was invited to Hogwarts,

Petunia applied for admission there as well, but was told that she would not be allowed to attend since she was not born with magical ability. Her sister, because of an innate magical ability, is treated as something special, praised by their parents, and then ultimately separated from Petunia. Petunia's response is to turn her hurt into contempt for all wizards. This is typical of prejudice. We see someone who has an ability we covet, but when we cannot obtain the same ability, we mentally turn things around in our mind and treat the other as a "freak." It preserves the self-centered ego, in other words, to treat the special abilities of others with disdain. In addition, Petunia's loss of companionship with her sister intensifies her disdain for those who are different, blaming them for the loss of that companionship. It's a typical selfish attitude where the actions of others are evaluated only in terms of how they affect oneself, without regard for what is best for another. Petunia's attitudes express a simple but powerful theme. Put simply, self-centered ego leads to prejudice and prejudice leads to misery for oneself and others.

The prejudice of some Muggles, exemplified by the Dursleys, is mirrored by the attitudes of some wizards. We encounter this first in the character of Draco Malfoy. As we later learn, Draco is the son of a powerful, wealthy, aristocratic wizard family and has been indoctrinated his whole life to believe in the innate superiority of pure-blood wizards. In their first encounter, Draco remarks to Harry, "They're just not the same, they've never been brought up to know our ways." Draco's prejudice extends not just to Muggles but to other wizards as well. In their next encounter on the train to Hogwarts, Draco tells Harry, "You'll soon find out some wizarding families are much better than others, Potter. You don't want to go making friends with the wrong sort."

Unlike Petunia Dursley, Draco's prejudice is not a result of jealousy for the ability of others, but results from indoctrinated disdain for those he considers of lesser heritage. The Malfoys are typical of the followers of Voldemort; they want to rid the world of those they regard as "mudbloods." This represents the all too common attitude of racial prejudice. It is a prejudice born out of false pride. The truth is that in *Harry Potter*, the muggle-born wizards and half-blood wizards are every bit as capable as the pure-blood wizards, but the pure-blood wizards' prejudice blinds them to this fact. In order to maintain their sense of superiority, they must resort to invention and lies. In *The Deathly Hallows*, after the followers of Voldemort have seized control of the Ministry of Magic, they begin making the claim that muggle-born and half-blood wizards must steal knowledge of magic from the pure-bloods. That claim blatantly ignores the truth in order to preserve the self-serving claims of the pure-bloods. As Ron Weasley says, "It's mental." In other words, racial prejudice is insane, but those who believe that way must preserve their false pride by inventing even more incredible lies and seeking to destroy those who would show the lie for what it is.

We find another example of prejudice in the character of Severus Snape, although it is not immediately apparent that it is prejudice. From their first encounter, Snape treats Harry with disdain. He demands that Harry be far better than the other students, and when Harry cannot live up to those expectations, Snape berates and dismisses Harry, often giving him much lower marks than Harry deserves. Yet, from time to time we see Snape working diligently in the background to help and guard Harry. Snape turns out to be the most complex and ambiguous character in the entire story. His behavior towards Harry is sometimes kind, sometimes inordinately harsh, and seems to have no rhyme or reason to it.

As the story unfolds over the course of the seven books, the motivation for Snape's behavior towards Harry is slowly revealed. First we find that Snape was at school with Harry's parents, James and Lily. But where Snape and James were continuously at odds with each other, Snape and Lily had been close friends and companions since childhood. What is first only hinted at becomes explicit in the seventh book. Snape has always been in love with Lily, and her choice to marry Snape's enemy James Potter will drive Snape to a horrible act of betrayal. Thinking that he can get rid of James and have Lily to himself, Snape reveals the prophecy about Harry to Voldemort. But Snape's plan backfires and Lily, not Harry, is the one who is killed. Snape's subsequent remorse leads to his activities as a double agent for Dumbledore, but also leaves him a tortured soul.

In light of Snape's history, we can understand Snape's attitudes toward Harry. He sees in Harry a combination of James and Lily. The image of James is despicable to Snape, but his love for Lily drives him to always seek to protect her child. It is the only way Snape can hope to redeem himself. Snape's actions toward Harry have very little to do with Harry, but are motivated by his own projection of attitudes about Harry's parents onto Harry combined with his own vow to help Dumbledore. It is another example of prejudice somewhat similar to that of Petunia Dursley. In the case of Snape, prejudice is born from jealousy and loss of love. It tortures his soul and manifests itself in the form of prejudice towards another, sometimes harmful and sometimes beneficial. Snape's prejudice blinds him to the true character of Harry such that he helps out of obligation, but never comes to know Harry.

Harry responds to Snape's disdain with his own prejudicial attitudes towards Snape. Because he does not understand why Snape treats him so harshly, Harry merely assumes that Snape is working for Voldemort and against Harry. Hagrid and Dumbledore's reassurances notwithstanding, Harry does not trust Snape, and that mistrust seems to be justified. However, Harry's prejudice towards Snape causes him and his friends to miss important clues and make nearly fatal mistakes beginning with *The Sorcerer's Stone* and continuing through to *The Deathly Hallows*. Harry also misses the opportunity to protect his mind from intrusion when he stops taking Occlumancy lessons from Snape. Harry's disdain for Snape and Snape's disdain for Harry make it impossible for them to work together, even though both would potentially benefit from that cooperation. Prejudice, by blinding us to the truth, causes us to miss beneficial opportunities.

This same cyclic prejudice shows up in the character of Riddle/Voldemort. As Riddle explains to Harry in *The Chamber of Secrets*:

> "You think I was going to use my filthy Muggle father's name forever? I, in whose veins runs the blood of Salazar Slytherin himself, through my mother's side? I, keep the name of a foul, common Muggle, who abandoned me even before I was born, just because he found out his wife was a witch? No, Harry – I fashioned myself a new name, a name I knew wizards everywhere would one day fear to speak, when I had become the greatest sorcerer in the world!"

Voldemort combines the dual aspects of prejudice we see in others. He has the racial prejudice of the pure-blood wizard combined with the hurt of having been abandoned. His father's rejection leads to his complementary disdain for Muggles. His pride of his mother's heritage combines with that disdain and turns inward to produce a blind arrogance where his only desire is to be considered the most powerful and feared wizard in the world.

Voldemort is the epitome of pride and prejudice and its danger. His political program, gathering him followers and increasing his power, is based on feeding prejudicial attitudes. He promises his followers that they will eliminate the "mudbloods" from the wizarding society and then rule over the non-magical Muggles as all-powerful tyrants. But, throughout the story, Voldemort is just as likely to turn on his followers and destroy them when they disappoint or fail in their missions. Voldemort's prejudice is not just against those who are different, but against anyone who stands in his way. His pride has consumed him to the point where it is only Voldemort that counts for anything, and others are only valuable to the extent they serve his needs.

There are other examples of prejudicial attitudes and behavior in *Harry Potter*, but these few examples are enough to make the point. What we see in all of these situations is the vicious cycle of destruction that arises from prejudice of all kinds. One person's prejudice leads to harm of another, and that harm leads to prejudicial blindness in regards to others as well. Ultimately, prejudice is an outgrowth of false pride, jealousy of those who are stronger and disdain for those who are weaker. Arrogant false pride strives to find something of lesser value to compare itself to and will imagine another to be lower in value if need be. Its central characteristic is that it is always self-serving at the expense of others. Prejudice, born out of pride, grows on irrational hatred towards others in order to justify its own self-centered desires. It blinds one to the truth, and ultimately leads to destruction. Pride goeth before a fall.

Nurture, Nature and Personal Choice

A long-standing debate about our human condition argues over the relative importance of nurture vs. nature. Are we good or evil because of something inherent? Do we become good or evil because of the influences on us during our life? Or, is good and evil a matter of personal choice?

Magical ability in the world of *Harry Potter* is an inborn ability. A person can improve that ability through study and practice, but cannot create it when it is not already there. This expresses one side of the debate. If nature does not give you an ability you cannot otherwise acquire it. An athletic ability falls into this category. Those of us born short and broad will never be able to dunk a basketball no matter how much we practice. The same is true of the voice and hearing abilities of an opera singer, or the eyesight and reflexes of a pilot. If we don't have it, we cannot get it by learning.

The question arises as to whether or not an inborn nature applies to things other than physical abilities. Does it also apply to virtue? In one sense, the *Harry Potter* books imply that it does. The students are sorted into houses according to the various virtues of courage, loyalty, intelligence, and cunning. There is even the implication that since all Death Eaters came from Slytherin, the instinct for good or evil is somehow innate. But by the end of the story, we find that is not the case. As Harry reveals to his son, "The Sorting Hat takes your choice into account."

The sorting of students into houses at Hogwarts doesn't imply that our lives are pre-ordained to follow a specific pattern, nor does it imply that one ability is superior to another. What the houses and sorting of students represents is the complementary nature of our abilities. Some will have a greater ability at acts that require courage, while others will have a greater interest in learning, etc. When we discover our native abilities and organize our lives accordingly, we will have a better chance at success. Furthermore, the combination of the talents of individuals creates a stronger whole. When each of us concentrates on what we are best suited to do, not only the individual but the whole society benefits.

The sorting of students into houses is parallel to the question of heritage. In many of the conversations among the students, they compare their house with those of their parents. It seems that certain qualities run in the family, as we say. All of the Weasley's are Gryffndors. All of the Blacks, with the exception of Sirius, are Slytherin. On the surface at least, it seems that natural ability and therefore influence is based on heritage, not choice. But, as Dumbledore explains, "It is our choices, Harry, that show what we truly are, far more than our abilities."

Thus, choice overrides nature, but that still leaves the question of nurture to consider. How much influence do others have on our behavior? If we compare Tom Riddle to Harry there are a good number of parallels. Both come from mixed-blood families, both were orphaned as children, and both had to grow up ignorant of their innate abilities. Overall, however, Voldemort had the better environment since the adults at the orphanage treated him far better than the Dursleys treated Harry. However, regardless of the care he received, Riddle turned early on to theft, deceit and cruelty towards other children. Despite that early step towards immoral behavior, Dumbledore invites him to Hogwarts and it appears Riddle was given all the care and concern that the other students receive from the teachers. Yet, Riddle slowly but surely turns toward evil.

There is a complementary example in the Weasley family. This family is probably the most loving and nurturing of all those we find in the books. Though poor, and of low social standing among pure-blood wizards, Mr. and Mrs. Weasley provide a comfortable and loving home to their seven children. Among their children we find a wide variety of attitudes and behavior. There is the pompous Percy, and the two lovable but irritatingly mischievous twins, George and Fred. Last of all is Ginny, whose innocent curiosity overcomes her upbringing. Her parents' influence failed to protect her from the diary planted on her by Lucius Malfoy. The evil in the book overcomes her free will, and she ends up committing horrendous acts that she never would have done otherwise. She all too easily falls into the trap set by Voldemort, despite her parents' warning. As Arthur Weasley reminds Ginny:

> "Haven't I taught you *anything?* What have I always told you? Never trust anything that can think for itself *if you can't see where it keeps its brain?* Why didn't you show the diary to me, or your mother?"

It seems that even the best nurturing by parents is not enough to always protect us from our own choices.

Another aspect to this debate is the influence of the diary and subsequent actions of Ginny. Like the *imperious* curse used by evil wizards to enslave another, it removes the person's free will. The loss of free will almost guarantees the person will act for the purposes of evil. Put another way, once an evil influence takes over, we can lose our ability to choose the good. We must, therefore, be cautious in what influences we allow in our lives. Our initial choice may be free, but once overpowered we can no longer choose freely and fall prey to domination by evil.

Ultimately good or evil is a matter of choice. We may be born with a nature that tends to evil, or we may be born with an instinct for good. We may also receive hard knocks that can become a pattern or excuse, or we can be raised by kind and loving adults. The books resolve this conflict by claiming that we are what we choose, not what we were born into or because of the influence of others no matter how strong those influences may be. As Rowling explained it in an interview:

> Harry is someone who is forced, for such a young person, to make his own choices. He has very limited access to truly caring adults and he is guided by his conscience. Now, Harry makes mistakes repeatedly. Harry did things like — he did steal the flying car. That was a very stupid thing to do, but it seemed like a great idea at the time. We've all been

there. But, ultimately Harry is guided by his conscience. [1]

We are all given an innate sense of conscience that can be further developed or not by the influences in our lives, but in the end we choose to listen to that inner voice, or we choose to reject it. That choice to rely on conscience sets apart the good from those who succumb to evil.

---

[1] J. K Rowling interview, The Connection (WBUR Radio), 12 October, 1999, http://www.accio-quote.org

Accepting the Consequences

Another important moral principle to consider is that we must be willing to accept the consequences of our mistakes. We will all eventually make poor moral choices, sometimes intentionally and sometimes unintentionally, sometimes with the best of motives and sometimes not. A major difference between a moral and immoral person is not that one never makes a poor choice and the other does, but that the moral person will always accept the consequences of his actions, even when he considers the actions justifiable.

In *The Sorcerer's Stone,* Harry, Ron and Hermione agree to help Hagrid get rid of the baby dragon that Hagrid has been raising. Hagrid never should have had the dragon in the first place, but his obsession with magical creatures sometimes overcomes good sense. He has drawn Harry and his friends into his little secret, and they are now trapped in a dilemma. If they go to the teachers and tell them what Hagrid has done, the dragon will probably be destroyed and Hagrid might lose his job. If they don't do anything, the dragon could be a danger to Hagrid and the students of Hogwarts. But trying to smuggle a live baby dragon out of Hogwarts is going to mean violating the rules. Yet, they decide to let their friendship override and agree to help. In the process, they get caught outside their rooms at night and have to face the consequences.

This time there is no excuse. Harry's other violations can often be justified on the grounds he was acting for good moral purposes. Trying to claim they were just sneaking a baby dragon off the grounds so that Hagrid wouldn't get in trouble isn't going to work. This time they have to accept the punishment without exception.

Even worse, because of the infraction, Harry's house is penalized severely in the house cup competition. It's not just Harry who suffers this time. All of his fellow students get punished indirectly. That's a good lesson to learn. It is not just ourselves that we have to worry about. We have to also worry about how our actions are going to affect others.

Getting caught and having to face the consequences of his actions forces Harry to stop and think, and he changes his attitude. For the rest of the year he avoids violating the school rules.

> It was a bit late to repair the damage, but Harry swore to himself not to meddle in things that weren't his business from now on. He'd had it with sneaking around and spying. He felt so ashamed of himself that he went to Wood and offered to resign from the Quidditch team.

Harry's attitude is one of remorse. It's not just the embarrassment of getting caught, and the fact that he is now treated badly by most of his fellow students. Harry has betrayed the trust of others, especially his fellow students.

Of course, this won't be the last time Harry goes out sneaking around, despite his intentions to play it safe from now on. There will be many times in the years to come when he has to go back to spying to find answers. This is part of growing up, too. Not every situation is one where we can ignore the rules. It takes a mature wisdom to understand the difference.

The important point in this episode is that Harry shows remorse. Later on, Hagrid also grieves that his carelessness led to a chain of events that nearly got Harry killed and nearly allowed Voldemort to return to power. We see remorse in Dumbledore as well when he admits that he has held knowledge back from Harry and when his own ego and desire causes him to be cursed by a Horcrux. That remorse is a sign of a moral conscience.

In contrast, remorse is something that Voldemort completely lacks. After killing Snape, "he turned away; there was no sadness in him, no remorse." Voldemort cannot comprehend that his actions are wrong, cannot have remorse, and so continues down the same path to destruction. Everything that goes wrong he considers someone else's failing and consequently keeps killing his own associates, weakening himself in the process.

We all make mistakes. That is an unfortunate reality of the human condition. What is important to realize is that mistakes can teach us things, but only if we are willing to accept the consequences of our mistakes. Hardening the heart against remorse in order to protect the ego only leads us to further mistakes.

History and Tradition

Hogwarts is a school with a rich history and tradition. Along with books in the library, much of that history is either hanging on the walls in the form of portraits or wandering the halls as ghosts. Unlike portraits in the Muggle world, these portraits can move around and talk. The people in the portraits can observe and comment on current events as well as describe historical events. The portraits, like the ghosts, are an interesting and inventive literary device. The portraits can provide clues to the heroes in the form of historical facts and in some cases can carry messages from one place to another. They also work as a metaphor of the importance of history and tradition.

In our quest for understanding of life we always have two important sources of information. Along with our own observations and experiences, we also have the knowledge of those who lived in the past. Our own experiences give us an understanding of the world we live in today. Because they are direct and personal, our experiences form the view of life we have. Living in the present we may not realize that those in the past have had many of the same problems that we face today and we can draw on history to help us in our understanding.

Although the technology, politics and social structures of man change through the centuries, human nature remains the same. The questions about life that we have today are the same questions and concerns that man has always had. We must decide what is good and what is evil, and then choose which we will live by. We have this mystery of life and death to consider as well. It is not necessary that we rediscover everything anew in each generation. Those who have come before have left their thoughts, their questions and answers for us to consider. We can learn from their successes and we can learn from their mistakes. But only if we are aware of history and study it can the lives of others be a benefit to us.

The portraits in the Hogwarts headmaster's office are a good example. The current headmaster has available to him all the knowledge and decisions of those who preceded him and he can turn to them for comment and advice when needed. Dumbledore does not always accept their opinion, however. When Phineas Black complains that you can't trust the students, Dumbledore tells him to be quiet.

Thus, although the voices that speak to us from the past can offer helpful advice, we must also know when to reject that advice. Human nature doesn't change, but the situations we find ourselves in do change. We must be careful not to get stuck in tradition just because it is tradition. We have to judge the present situation on its own merits, apply the traditions we have been taught, and the wisdom of others from the past, when they are appropriate and reject them when not.

The Riddle of Voldemort

The Dark Wizard Voldemort is the chief villain and opponent of Harry and the overall dramatic arc of the entire *Harry Potter* series is built on the conflict between them. The first book starts, and the final book concludes, with Voldemort's attempts to kill Harry. Throughout the whole saga we are faced with this riddle: why is Voldemort trying to kill Harry? Voldemort's very name symbolizes the riddle, and his character gives us understanding of the answer to the riddle.

In *The Chamber of Secrets* it is revealed that Voldemort is the last surviving heir of the house of Slytherin whose original name was Tom Marvolo Riddle. His surname Riddle comes from his Muggle father, one who abandoned Tom before birth. Out of hatred for the one who rejected him, he rejects that name, kills his father and adopts an anagram of his name, "I am Lord Voldemort." The name Voldemort was invented by Rowling from the French words *vol de mort* meaning "flight of death." Read abstractly, we can say that the flight of death is the nature of the riddle that must be solved. The riddle of Voldemort's evil and his continuing attack on Harry has something to do with death.

As we learn in the *Order of the Phoenix,* for Voldemort "there is nothing worse than death," and he will do whatever he must do to escape death. All of Voldemort's unspeakable acts are born out of a desire to gain power over death. He has discovered a form of magic that he believes will insure his own immortality. But, to become immortal, he must fracture his soul by committing murder and then store each soul fragment as a Horcrux. So long as even one of the Horcruxes remains, a portion of Voldemort's soul remains on earth and he cannot be killed. His body may become weakened, as it was during the first attack on Harry, but since his soul still remains on the earth, he can be physically restored.

Voldemort's obsession to avoid death is what ultimately corrupts him. In making that choice he abandons all compassion for others and seeks only those things that will serve his obsession. His goal of immortality requires destroying others, and that willingness to destroy others can only be achieved by so denigrating them that he cannot conceive of them as anything other than a means to an end. In short, he cannot love others and achieve his goal. By abandoning love he eventually becomes everything that is disgusting in human nature. He is filled with pride, prejudiced, self-centered, lying, merciless, and remorseless, caring for no one apart from himself except those who worship him, and those only so long as they serve his needs.

Ultimately, Voldemort abandons all sense of morality. As Professor Quirrell stated, "Lord Voldemort showed me how wrong I was. There is no good and evil, there is only power, and those too weak to seek it." Unfortunately for Quirrell, Voldemort "does not forgive mistakes easily" and Voldemort will sacrifice Quirrell to get what he wants. In fact, Voldemort will sacrifice anything other than himself, as when he demands that Pettigrew cut off his own hand to restore Voldemort's body. In his self-serving desire to live, he feeds on others, drawing what he needs and then discarding the remains. Simply put, in order to survive he becomes a parasite.

The nature of a parasite is that it can only live by taking life from another, even if it kills the host in the process. Voldemort will even sacrifice that which is innocent and pure. He attacks Harry as a baby, and uses young Ginny Weasley, both symbols of innocence. A shocking example of his destruction of innocence is in the scene involving the killing of a unicorn, another symbol of purity and innocence. The horror of that act is explained to Harry by the centaur Firenze:

> "Only one who has nothing to lose, and everything to gain, would commit such a crime. The blood of a unicorn will keep you alive, even if you are an inch from death, but at a terrible price. You have slain something pure and defenseless to save yourself, and you will have but a half-life, a cursed life, from the moment the blood touches your lips."

When Voldemort discovers there is a prophecy that a boy born recently will be a threat to him, Voldemort's obsession drives him to destroy that threat. Once again, it is Voldemort's self-serving obsession with immortality that provides the key to understand the riddle of his repeated attacks on Harry.

Harry's only hope, it seems, is to kill Voldemort first and that is the reason for his quest to destroy the Horcruxes. Until all the Horcruxes are located and destroyed, Voldemort cannot be killed. Thus, Harry must seek out and destroy them if he is to live. However, just as Voldemort will destroy anything to reach his goal, he will likewise seek to destroy anything that interferes with that goal. Thus, Voldemort protects each Horcrux with curses and anyone who tries to destroy a Horcrux can become cursed. Dumbledore's mishandling of a Horcrux is one example. To even attempt to defeat Voldemort means touching something inherently evil and possibly becoming corrupt in the process. Nevertheless, the destruction of the Horcurxes is the task that Harry must undertake if he is to defeat the evil directed against him. This is a part of the riddle as well. We cannot run from evil, but must confront it if we are to overcome and survive. Yet, when confronting evil, we must be careful that we do not become the thing we oppose.

There is another aspect of Voldemort's name that symbolizes the nature of the riddle. Riddle's first name, Tom, is an abbreviated form of Thomas and means "twin." Although not immediately apparent, Voldemort is a symbolic twin of Harry. As the story unfolds we discover there is a link between Voldemort and Harry. The scar on Harry's forehead blinds him with pain when he is near Voldemort. In addition, Harry can sometimes see what Voldemort is doing. Harry eventually discovers the truth. When Voldemort attempted to kill Harry as a boy, a piece of Voldemort's weakened soul fractured and lodged within Harry. The piece of Voldemort inside gives Harry a dual nature, part himself and part Voldemort. When Voldemort restores his body using Harry's blood, Voldemort likewise takes a piece of Harry into himself. Each carries a piece of the other within, and their destinies are forever tied together as the prophecy about Harry states. The linkage between Harry and Voldemort is a key piece of the riddle that is Voldemort and seeing that link is essential to understanding the conflict that must be resolved in the story. Until the link is broken, Harry cannot be free.

Voldemort does not truly understand this connection, however. He thinks that the connection is to his advantage and seeks to use it to destroy Harry during the confrontation at the end of *The Order of the Phoenix.* The attempt fails, but proves the connection exists. As Dumbledore explains to Harry,

> "Voldemort's aim in possessing you, as he demonstrated tonight, would not have been my destruction. It would have been yours. He hoped, when he possessed you briefly a short while ago, that I would sacrifice you in the hope of killing him."

Once again, the evil that Voldemort represents acts as a parasite. It seeks to destroy by possession. Metaphorically, Harry carries a fragment of evil within that by possessing him seeks to destroy.

Looking at the character of Voldemort we see a personification of evil. Voldemort puts himself and his desires above all else, he seeks his own immortality and complete dominion over others. Simply put, he has no love for anything but himself. This is the answer to the riddle. Evil knows no love, thinks only of itself, and fears death.

As he is a personification of evil, it is tempting to treat Voldemort as an allegorical Satan. The symbolism attached to Voldemort certainly points in that direction. As an heir of Slytherin, Voldemort can speak *parseltounge,* the language of serpents, and the coat of arms for Slytherin is a silver snake on a green field. Voldemort's familiar, and one of the Horcruxes, is the snake Nagini. Voldemort, as Tom Riddle, also controls the Basilisk, a large serpent. Even Voldemort's appearance is that of a snake, with red slit-like eyes and a snake-like nose. However, beyond that association with a serpent, there is little to make him a direct symbol of Satan. Voldemort is a mortal being who is seeking knowledge to become immortal. That is not an allegory of Satan, but it is familiar to those who know the Bible. Consider the temptation of Adam and Eve as described in Genesis chapter three:

Now the serpent was more shrewd than any of the wild animals that the Lord God had made. He said to the woman, "Is it really true that God said, 'You must not eat from any tree of the orchard'?" The woman said to the serpent, "We may eat of the fruit from the trees of the orchard; but concerning the fruit of the tree that is in the middle of the orchard God said, 'You must not eat from it, and you must not touch it, or else you will die.'" The serpent said to the woman, "Surely you will not die, for God knows that when you eat from it your eyes will open and you will be like divine beings who know good and evil." (Genesis 3:1-5)

Voldemort cannot easily be made into a literary symbol of Satan, but he is an accurate representation of fallen man. He hears the voice of the serpent and seeks knowledge of good and evil to obtain the ability to be like God with power over life and death. Once man steps over the boundaries set by God and seeks to become as God, man descends into evil. He no longer has the connection to a divine guidance that will give him knowledge of good and evil, but seeks to determine good and evil for himself, and eventually discards any distinction between good and evil. Lacking the true source of life, fallen man must rely on the blood of others for life. This is represented in Genesis by God's killing of animals to obtain clothing for Adam and Eve, and the continued sacrifice of animals that man may live. In that fallen condition, there is no depth to which fallen man cannot sink. The end result is a nature summed up by Proverbs 6:16-19:

There are six things that the Lord hates, even seven things that are an abomination to him: haughty eyes, a lying tongue, and hands that shed innocent blood, a heart that devises wicked plans, feet that are swift to run to evil, a false witness who pours out lies, and a person who spreads discord among family members.

Once man rebels against God, man has become enslaved to evil. Remember that Harry carries a fragment of Voldemort in his scar.

Symbolically, evil has embedded itself in Harry's mind. That is the Biblical view of mankind, the riddle of evil that man does not want to look at, for it means that each of us is a potential Voldemort. Each has within him the nature of evil in the form of sin and rebellion to God, and that evil can and will kill us given a chance. Until that evil nature is removed, we can never truly live.

The Undying Power of Love

Set against the self-serving cruelty of Voldemort is the self-denying love of those that oppose him. Their actions initiated by love, from the beginning of the story to the end, will thwart Voldemort's attempts at complete mastery of his destiny. In the first episode, Voldemort's attempt to kill Harry as a boy was blocked by Lily Potter's intervention. Voldemort had sought to get Lily to step aside, a very out-of-character act that is only explained near the end of the saga, but Lily voluntarily stood in front of Harry while Voldemort killed her. There is no indication that she even tried to fight back. That act of self-sacrifice born out of love gave Harry protection against Voldemort's death curse and it was Voldemort, not Harry, who was harmed by the curse. As Dumbledore explained:

> "Your mother died to save you. If there is one thing Voldemort cannot understand, it is love. He didn't realize that love as powerful as your mother's for you leaves its mark. Not a scar, no visible sign … to have been loved so deeply, even though the person who loved us is gone, will give some protection forever."

Lily's act of love gives Harry immediate protection from Voldemort, but as Dumbledore explains later in the story, the sacrifice of Lily and her blood relation to Petunia Dursley seals the protection that Dumbledore places on the Dursley's residence and gives Harry an on-going protection. No curse that Voldemort can throw is powerfully enough to overcome the love that protects Harry, and this fact becomes important to the story's development.

Dobby the house-elf is another character that benefits Harry by his love. Dobby's attempts at protecting Harry in *The Chamber of*

Secrets are a little misguided and create more problems than they solve. Yet, since he must punish himself every time he acts for Harry's benefit, Dobby's love is in the same category as Lily's. His actions for Harry's benefit cost him, yet he does not hold back. Harry grows fond of Dobby by the end of the episode, but realizing Dobby doesn't always do the wise thing, asks him to "Just promise never to try and save my life again." Dobby, however, ignores Harry's request. Dobby's love for Harry is too strong, and when Harry is imprisoned in the cellar of the Malfoy house, it is Dobby who comes to Harry's rescue. That act of love costs Dobby his life. Yet, in that tragic loss, Harry learns something very important:

> He had learned control at last, learned to shut his mind to Voldemort, the very thing Dumbledore had wanted him to learn from Snape. Just as Voldemort had not been able to posses Harry while Harry was consumed with grief for Sirius, so his thoughts could not penetrate Harry now, while he mourned Dobby. Grief, it seemed, drove Voldemort out...though Dumbledore, of course, would have said that it was love....

Digging Dobby's grave, with Dobby's blood still on his hands, Harry finally reaches a turning point in his quest. He has discovered that love will break the connection with Voldemort and prevent Harry from being distracted by Voldemort's schemes. Once again, it is love that triumphs over Voldemort's magical abilities.

The idea that love is more powerful than any other magic is another important theme in the story and ultimately is key to the resolution of the plot. To understand the magic of *Harry Potter* and how Harry has a "power the Dark Lord knows not" requires understanding the nature of self-sacrifice done out of love.

We can start by looking at Lily's action in purely human terms as it is a good analogy to the actions of parents towards their children. A parent must sacrifice for the children in many ways, giving of their time, money, and guidance so that the child will be prepared for life. That preparation for life can remain with us even when our parents are gone. Self-sacrificing love as a theme in *Harry Potter* is not limited to just parents and their children, however. There are many other characters in *Harry Potter* who express the same attitude without any blood relation at all. Thus, the love that is key to the plot is not simply love for close relations, but a more general and widely applicable kind of love.

When we talk about how we love something we often mean it in a self-centered way. We often love someone because we admire who they are or what they do, or because they do something that gives us joy, physical comfort, or satisfies out desires. So often, when people say, "I love you" the emphasis seems to be on the "I" part – *I* love you because of what you do for *me*. However, a love that is based on what the other person is or does is prone to failure. After all, eventually we will discover that the other person is not perfect, does some things or believes some things that we cannot accept. Do you stop loving the person at that point? If the love we have for another is based on admirable traits in that person, that love can fail the moment we discover the other person also has some not-so-admirable traits. We can say that it is a conditional love.

Conditional love is explored in *Harry Potter* as well. It shows up in the relationships between Harry, Ron and Hermione. At times they come to sharp disagreements over how they should respond to the problems they face. At other times there is a spark of jealousy that flares up into bitterness. These lead to on-again-off-again places in their friendship, but at each stage they reconcile, learning that loving someone goes beyond just finding that person agreeable. It is part of their process of maturing throughout the story and disagreements are handled better each time.

This conditional love, a love that exists in response to something that is worth loving, is typically what people mean by love. When we find something beautiful, admirable, compatible with us, that gives us joy, it is natural and expected to love that thing. So, it's not all bad to love that way, and it's a good place to start. The problem is that it is a love that can fail, leaving us with a sense of unrequited love, emotional pain, disappointment and even despair.

That is the situation we see in Snape's love for Lily. He admires her both for her talent and for her companionship, for her respect for him, and perhaps because she shows him a love in return that Snape does not get otherwise. Snape's love, however, turns against him when Lily marries James Potter. Snape's disdain for James and his desire for Lily causes him to commit an act of betrayal. He reveals the prophecy spoken about Voldemort in return for Voldemort's promise to let Lily live. This is the source of Voldemort's out-of-character action when he tells Lily to step aside. It is not compassion on Voldemort's part, but part of an agreement, and one that is easily abandoned. Snape's self-serving love for Lily backfires and leaves Snape forever without the one he loves. Yet, Snape comes to understand something from this. His remorse gives him the understanding he needs that will lead him to work for Harry's protection and Dumbledore's plan, even though doing so puts Snape in danger and eventually costs him his life also.

In maturing from adolescence to manhood, this is the lesson that Harry must learn. It is in Harry's nature to be the hero for those suffering injustice, but there is another aspect of his nature that must be developed. He must learn to have compassion and concern, even for those who would be his enemy. We see this in Harry's relationship to Kreacher, the house-elf. Kreacher is the one who was instrumental in the events that led up to Sirius Black's death and Harry's near fatal encounter with Voldemort at the Ministry of Magic. Sirius was Harry's godfather, a link to his father and mother, and had become Harry's friend and protector. Sirius's death is nearly the moment of failure for Harry. He feels responsible and is ready to give it all up. Dumbledore explains that, although Harry's actions played a part, it was Voldemort's manipulation and Kreacher's betrayal that resulted in Sirius's death, not Harry. With Sirius's death Harry becomes the owner of the Black estate, including control over the house-elf Kreacher. It is within Harry's power to treat Kreacher cruelly, but with the warning of Dumbledore and the encouragement of Hermione, Harry does the opposite. Through acts of compassion and kindness Harry wins Kreacher's support. It is Kreacher who locates the missing locket containing one of the Horcruxes, an important step leading to the defeat of Voldemort.

Harry also learns that it isn't just his friends and those that can serve him that deserve compassion. During the battle for Hogwarts, there is a moment where Draco is trapped by an unquenchable fire. Harry has already acquired his own means of escape, yet he turns around and rescues Draco. Draco has never shown any love towards Harry and in fact has just been trying to capture Harry to gain Voldemort's approval. Harry's act, putting him in danger, is an act of compassion for an enemy. That act of compassion is rewarded later in the Forbidden Forest when it is Draco's mother that lies to protect Harry. He is the one who has given her hope of seeing her son again, and even for one of Voldemort's Death Eaters, her love for her son is stronger that Voldemort can imagine.

Many have died to protect Harry, and in the end that knowledge forces him to make a choice. He can continue the battle while others die, or he can act in self-sacrificing love to stop the killing. Having known love, Harry responds with love and goes to face Voldemort alone and undefended. In so doing, he will ultimately defeat Voldemort. In their final confrontation, Harry shows the greatest act of compassion of all. He tries to warn Voldemort, to stop him from a final act of evil and destruction, and urges Voldemort to find remorse. When Voldemort's shouts his *Avada Kerdavra* curse Harry responds only with *Expelliarmus*, a disarming spell. Harry has reached the point where he no longer seeks vengeance, but mercy, and desires to disarm Voldemort rather than destroy him. Of course, it is too late for Voldemort despite Harry's compassion.

In contrast, even though he is aware of what he is up against, Voldemort does not, in fact cannot understand the nature of love. As he explained to his Death Eaters, "This is old magic, I should have remembered it, I was foolish to overlook it." Yet, despite admitting the power in that act of love, Voldemort cannot truly comprehend it and his lack of understanding will be his downfall. Never having known love, he cannot understand its power. Dumbledore explains this to Harry:

> "But I knew too where Voldemort was weak. And so I made my decision. You would be protected by an ancient magic of which he knows, which he despises, and which he has always, therefore, underestimated – to his cost. I am speaking, of course, of the fact that your mother died to save you. She gave you a lingering protection he never expected, a protection that flows in your veins to this day. I put my trust, therefore, in your mother's blood."

Notice also how Dumbledore links love to blood. Blood is the symbol of life, and to kill is to shed blood. Because Harry has the blood of the one that loved him enough to die for him he is protected. In *The Sorcerer's Stone,* Voldemort cannot even touch Harry. Later, after his revival in *The Goblet of Fire* by taking some of Harry's blood, Voldemort can touch Harry. The "magic" of sacrificial love is linked to taking the blood of the one who dies.

This power in love was foretold in the prophecy about Harry where it states, "He will have power the Dark Lord knows not." That power is what protected Harry from beginning to end. Yet, even after Voldemort has failed to kill Harry in numerous attempts because of the power of that love, Voldemort still cannot understand. His pride combines with his ignorance such that he treats the self-sacrificing love of Harry, Lily, Dobby, Dumbledore and Snape, with disdain.

> "Is it love again?" said Voldemort, his snake's face jeering. "Dumbledore's favorite solution, *love,* which he claimed conquered death, though love did not stop him falling from the tower and breaking like and old waxwork? *Love,* which did not prevent me stamping out your Mudblood mother like a cockroach, Potter – and nobody seems to love you enough to run forward this time and take my curse. So what will stop you dying now when I strike?"

Yes, Harry tells him, and even more than that. That power, that magic greater than Voldemort can understand, already resides in Harry and it has grown past the point where Voldemort can defeat it. The thing that protects Harry from being overcome and possessed by Voldemort, and the thing that prevents Voldemort from killing Harry, is the thing that Voldemort does not understand. Love. Without the sacrificial love of another, Harry would never have survived the evil that attached itself to him. For Harry to rid himself and others of evil required an act equal to the love that protected him.

There are those who will say that love is a universal virtue in mankind and these images of sacrificial love are likewise universal. While that is true, what often appears as sacrificial love contains a portion of self-serving attitude. There are heroes of history, myth and literature who give up life rather than back down from danger and conflict. They may also sacrifice themselves rather than live without those they love. Usually the dying hero is overcome by greater power or through betrayal but fights until the very end. Thus, we admire the hero because of his courage and tenacity. However, his sacrifice still contains an element that is self-serving. The hero understands that he must die at some point in life but would rather die valiantly, resisting evil, than be thought of as a coward or a weakling. It is sacrificial, but it is also self serving. The hero expects to be remembered as valiant, or perhaps to gain a reward in an afterlife, and that is his motivation for sacrifice. More importantly, the sacrificial act provides a protection for others, but does not extend beyond the death of the hero.

There is something in *Harry Potter* that goes beyond the world's idea of love and sacrifice. It is not immediately obvious, but what the story describes is the love that is central to Christianity. Jesus said to his disciples, "No one has greater love than this – that one lays down his life for his friends" (John 15:13). Like a mythical hero, Jesus was betrayed and taken by a greater power, or so it seemed. What the Gospel states, however, is that Jesus was well aware of the betrayer and allowed him to act (John 13:21-30). When the soldiers came to arrest Jesus, he did not resist and prevented his own disciples from acting on his behalf (John 18:10-11). When put on trial, Jesus did not defend himself. As Jesus had previously stated, "No one takes [life] from me, but I lay it down of my own free will" (John 10:18). When questioned by Pilate, Jesus said, "You would have no authority over me at all, unless it was given to you from above" (John 19:11). This is an important difference between Jesus and the typical hero of myth. Jesus expresses a love for others and a willingness to die without defending himself, knowing that his voluntary sacrifice is the only way evil can be defeated.

We see the same act of voluntary sacrifice by the characters in *Harry Potter*. Lily does not defend herself against Voldemort, has the opportunity to step aside, but refuses to do so. Dobby has every excuse to avoid helping wizards, but sacrifices himself nonetheless. Dumbledore also stands defenseless, voluntarily allowing himself to be killed by Snape. Even Snape shows the same action. He places himself near Voldemort, but never attempts to kill Voldemort and in the end is struck down. Harry likewise stands before Voldemort in the Forbidden Forest and accepts death without resistance in order that evil may be destroyed. As Jesus stood before Pilate, refusing to defend himself, the heroes in *Harry Potter* do the same. Surprising to Harry, his sacrifice of himself does not result in his death. He comes to understand the true relationship of love and sacrifice. Because Harry did not defend himself, but was willing to die so that others may live, he reawakens with the fragment of Voldemort gone forever. It is in that new state that Harry can now defeat Voldemort.

Many people, even those who are not professing Christians, are familiar with John 3:16: "For this is the way God loved the world: He gave his one and only Son, so that everyone who believes in him will not perish but have eternal life." What must also be understood is that the sacrifice of Jesus results in more than his dying; it also results in His resurrection. The love of Jesus for mankind did not end with His death, but returned in even greater power at His resurrection. Just as Harry learns that love can drive Voldemort from his mind, the power of the death and resurrection drives sin from man. Remember also that the "magic" in love is linked to having the blood of the one who died. That is also a central symbol of Christianity. Jesus said, "The one who eats my flesh and drinks my blood resides in me, and I in him" (John 6:56). That power of the resurrection not only removes sin, but provides for the regeneration of all those who believe, those who take within the body and blood of Christ.

To be clear, the story in *Harry Potter* is not a direct allegory of the life, death and resurrection of Jesus, and we should not stretch the meaning beyond what is in the story, as much as some might like to. Harry is not Christ any more than Lily, Dumbledore, Dobby or Snape. Harry must be helped by others, and must grow into his understanding of the nature and power of sacrificial love. By the end of the story, Harry has progressed from a hot-tempered, impatient and imprudent youth to an adult with a mature level of understanding that gives him the ability to overcome evil. Harry is better seen as the personification of the life of a Christian. He is a pilgrim on a journey of sanctification, following the same path that Jesus walked. As Jesus said, anyone who would be His disciple must "Deny himself, take up your cross, and follow me" (Matthew 16:24). That is what the disciples of Jesus must do. That is a good analogy of what Harry did. The characters in the story are "Christ-like" but not Christ and sacrificial love is thematic.

Love as portrayed in *Harry Potter* expresses a core doctrine of Christianity. Summarized, it states that there is a power in love that can transcend any evil, offer protection from death, and does not disappear with the death of the one who loves. Furthermore, it is a love that is offered not just to those who benefit us, but equally to all, including our enemies. That is the love that God shows to man in the Gospel of Jesus Christ. The characters in the story must come to this knowledge, and they do so through experience not just intellectually. So also it is for all of those who follow Jesus as disciples. All who follow Jesus come to understand the "greater magic" that is described in *Harry Potter*. Sacrificial love releases an on-going protection. It is a power that does not cease with the one who died, but rather it is an undying power of love.

Conquering Death

There are many themes in *Harry Potter,* but all the themes are woven together like a tapestry. The threads intertwine and crisscross each other such that if you follow any one of them it will eventually intersect with the main thread. That one thread that runs from beginning to end in *Harry Potter* concerns conquering death. Throughout the story the question of death is central and different views on conquering death compete with each other, offering the reader a variety of answers. At the beginning and again at the end, Harry finds there is only one true answer. He also finds that the answer is a paradox.

In *The Chamber of Secrets* Voldemort states that his desire was to become so powerful that others would fear to speak his name. As Voldemort means "flight of death" to fear to speak his name is a fear to speak of death. Just as we use euphemisms for death, such as passed on, passed away, or no longer with us, the wizards only speak of You-Know-Who, He-Who-Must-Not-be-Named, or simply the Dark Lord. When Harry speaks Voldemort's name without hesitation, the others around him cringe and berate him. But, like Harry, Dumbledore is not afraid of using Voldemort's name. At the end of *The Sorcerer's Stone* he tells Harry, "Always use the proper name for things. Fear of a name increases fear of the thing itself." This is an important first step in conquering death. We must not fear to speak of it or call it what it is. As Dumbledore tells Harry, "After all, to the well-organized mind, death is but the next great adventure."

It is his fear of death that drives Voldemort to seek a means of becoming immortal and invincible. "There is nothing worse than death" is Voldemort's belief. To that end he fractures his soul and stores the fragments in the Horcruxes, protecting each with a curse. So long as one fragment of his soul remains, Voldemort is tethered to life. In so doing, he believes he has conquered death. The double flaw in his plan is that the Horcruxes can be found and destroyed, and although he cannot be killed, he can be diminished to a mere vapor. That is what happened in Voldemort's first attempt to kill Harry. The Horcruxes require abominable acts in their creation and are never foolproof. The one who seeks to conquer death by this means can never be free to live. He must always be on guard, must seek ever greater power and ultimately has not conquered death at all. His fear of death has conquered him instead, determining his course through life.

Voldemort is not the only one who seeks to conquer death. As a young man, Dumbledore also sought that end. Unlike Voldemort, Dumbledore studied and sought out the Deathly Hallows. At some point in his life Dumbledore encounters each one, but none of them provides the solution that he seeks. Worse, Dumbledore's desire for the Hallows gets him involved with Grindelwald, a forerunner of Voldemort. Dumbledore and Grindelwald sought the Deathly Hallows, but sought them for power. Their search and Dumbledore's desires for power result in tragedy when Dumbledore's sister is killed. That death changed Dumbledore's attitudes, and he no longer sought power in the same way again, giving up his quest for the Hallows. Harry faces a similar choice. He can seek the Hallows in hopes of gaining power, or he can seek the Horcruxes in the hope of destroying evil. Harry chooses the wiser path of finding and destroying the Horcruxes. Yet the Hallows and the Horcruxes will intersect in the final battle of Hogwarts. Having sought the right thing, Harry obtains both. In so doing, he will come to understand what it means to conquer death.

There are three Deathly Hallows, the Elder Wand, the Resurrection Stone, and the Cloak of Invisibility, each of which represents a possible means of conquering death. The three Hallows are described in the *Tale of the Three Brothers*, a wizard children's story embedded within *Harry Potter and the Deathly Hallows*.

The first of the Hallows is the Elder Wand. It is "a wand more powerful than any in existence: a wand that must always win duels for its owner, a wand worthy of a wizard who had conquered Death." The second of the Hallows is a stone having "the power to recall others from Death." The third of the Hallows is Death's "own Cloak of Invisibility" and allows the owner to "go forth…without being followed by Death." Each of the three objects describes a way that men have sought to conquer death.

The Elder Wand represents conquering death by making the possessor invincible. As such, it represents power to resist death. Its flaw is that the possessor soon becomes careless, and the jealousy of others will eventually cause them to kill the owner at the first moment he has become vulnerable. The wand's power does not truly conquer death, only postpones it and only so long as the owner maintains his vigilance. We can see in the Elder Wand the solution that is most common in men's minds. They watch carefully over their health, avoid danger, and minimize risks, but eventually death catches up with them anyway. The most extreme form of this solution is that predicted by some today. They believe that with technology we can either remove the causes of death, or perhaps store consciousness in a machine and thus never die. As with the Elder Wand, resisting death by those means is only a hope and at best a temporary solution. Obviously, staying healthy and avoiding risk so as to be able to live life to its fullest is a wise choice. However, when we end up consuming life trying to resist death, never truly enjoying life as a result, we have not conquered death but become trapped by it. Seeking the Elder Wand becomes a fool's quest, yet one that many follow.

The resurrection stone represents conquering death by bringing the dead back to life. In the *Tale of the Three Brothers*, this turns into a trap. Although the holder of the stone can bring back the dead, they are not brought back to true physical life, but are separated by a veil. As a consequence, the mere image of those brought back by the stone leads to despair and eventually to the death of the holder of the stone. Those who dwell on the dead, endlessly longing for their return, can become trapped in depression and eventually despair. Despair leads to death, since the person no longer feels joy at living and ultimately has no life at all. In the worst case, despair leads to suicide. In another sense, the resurrection stone can represent those who consider their immortality to be held in memory by others still alive. Such a person can spend his whole life trying to do things that will live after he is gone. In the end, his life is consumed by fear of not being remembered and his choices in life are guided by that fear. Yet, even if a person achieves fame, his continued existence in the memories of others is only a phantom existence, not true life beyond death.

However, used wisely the resurrection stone does have an important power. When we think of those who are dead, bringing their lives to memory, their examples can be a benefit to us. For those who do not fear their own death, the comfort of others who have already gone beyond death can be a blessing rather than a curse. The examples of their lives are a means of avoiding despair rather than causing it. If they walked this earth, lived a full life, and embraced death when it came, then we have hope that we can do the same. This use of the Resurrection Stone is what allows Harry to pass by the Dementors on his way to confront Voldemort. The stone calls up shimmering images of those that he loves and have already passed from life to death. From their example he gains the peace he needs to avoid despair.

The Cloak of Invisibility is the most unusual of all the Hallows. It has the power to hide the person wearing it, and thus the person can avoid death in many situations. The puzzling part of the story is that the cloak is the one worn by Death. The wearer of the cloak is not visible to the living and thus, in effect, he takes on the form of death. And, having already cloaked himself in death, he can cast the cloak aside at anytime without fear of the consequences. This was the choice of the third brother in the tale, and he was praised by Death for his wisdom. One fairly obvious interpretation is that when we no longer fear death, having already embraced it, we can truly live. This is a paradox, to be sure, but a key element in understanding *Harry Potter*.

Dumbledore and Grindelwald considered the Cloak insignificant and did not even search for it. Since they could make themselves invisible, they did not consider the cloak as something that would increase their power. They fail to understand its power, in other words. Harry is the one who possesses the Cloak of Invisibility. When the time comes, he takes the cloak off, stands vulnerable in front of Voldemort, and is struck down as a consequence. In the visionary dream that follows, Dumbledore tells Harry,

> "You are the true master of death, because the
> true master does not seek to run away from Death.
> He accepts that he must die, and understands that

there are far, far worse things in the living world than dying."

Harry has learned the lessons of the Deathly Hallows and become the master of them. He did not seek the Elder Wand for power over others, and obtains it only to set it aside. He did not use the Resurrection Stone to bring back those at peace, but to enable his own self-sacrifice. He cast aside the Cloak of Invisibility when it was time to embrace his own death. There is one question remaining, however. What would lead a person to the point where he is willing to embrace death as a means of conquering death?

Harry's understanding did not come easily or quickly. It was the result of seven years of struggle, questioning, and searching for answers. He first comes to understand the need to pursue justice for others, even when it puts him at risk. In so doing he comes to understand that there are things worse than death. Turning to evil, or even allowing evil to exist in the world, solely to protect oneself is a life worse than death.

When he faces the Mirror of Erised and removes the Philosopher's stone, Harry demonstrates another important virtue. He does not seek power over death for himself. He can remove the stone from the mirror because he only wants to prevent it falling into the wrong hands. The destruction of the Philosopher's stone shows that continuation of physical existence alone is not the answer to conquering death.

Harry also learns the power of sacrificial love when his mother's death protects him from Voldemort's touch. Harry is protected because he carries the blood of the one who loved him enough to die for him. Later Harry learns another power of love. His love of others, shown in grieving for their deaths, protects his mind from being invaded by Voldemort. Harry also develops close friendships and learns to love others and be loved by them. His desire that they not die is part of his motivation for facing his own death. In the Triwizard tournament Harry rescues other students from under the water, putting his own life at risk, even though he was not required to do so. Later, he will not run from a confrontation with Voldemort since to do so would leave others to die in his place when he could have prevented their deaths through his own sacrifice.

Harry also grows in courage. It is the path he chose when he was sorted into Gryffindor. That choice was later shown to be accurate when he pulls the Sword of Gryffindor from the Sorting Hat in the *Chamber of Secrets*. He can pull the sword from the hat because he has maintained his courage and integrity in the face of death. To conquer death takes courage and integrity.

The wounds Harry suffers in fighting the Basilisk are cured by the tears of the Phoenix, a bird that has the power of resurrection, of being reborn in its death. In the battle at the Ministry of Magic, Harry sees the Phoenix swallow a curse intended for Dumbledore, dying because of it yet able to be reborn. Harry sees that there is a power from death that can protect and heal even the most serious wounds.

In his confrontations with the Dementors Harry learns the nature of despair, how it can destroy the soul of a person leaving a hollow shell. Physical life alone, without joy in the soul is torment and it is better to die than live that way. He also learns the means of conquering despair when he finds that memories of love and joy produce a force that drives back despair. Harry also avoids despair by understanding that there is life beyond death, that death is not the end, but only the beginning of "the next great adventure." He is reminded of this fact by Hermione when they stand in front of the Potter's tomb. Even so, Harry is nearly overcome by grief at by loss of those he loves. It is only later when he uses the Resurrection Stone to recall their images that the despair is driven away. Their transcendence of death gives him the hope he needs.

Above all else, Harry learns that it is virtue, not knowledge, not power that conquers death. At the battle in the Ministry of Magic, Harry is nearly possessed by Voldemort, but Voldemort's attempt fails. Had Voldemort taken control, he could have destroyed Harry. Dumbledore explains the reason Harry survived:

> "There is a room in the Department of Mysteries," interrupted Dumbledore, "that is kept locked at all times. It contains a force that is at once more wonderful and more terrible than death, than human intelligence, than forces of nature. It is also, perhaps, the most mysterious of the many subjects for study that reside there. It is the power held within

that room that you possess in such quantities and which Voldemort has not at all. That power took you to save Sirius tonight. That power also saved you from possession by Voldemort, because he could not bear to reside in a body so full of the force he detests. In the end, it matters not that you could not close your mind. It was your heart that saved you."

Whatever other failings he may have, Harry's heart is good. He has courage, compassion, humility, integrity, a desire for truth and justice, and above all love. When the inner man has become those things, evil cannot penetrate into the person's being, cannot bring about death of the soul. Thus, to drive out evil with good is to conquer death as well.

The link between Harry and Voldemort is the greatest challenge Harry faces. At the moment when Voldemort tried to kill the baby Harry, a fragment of Voldemort became lodged in Harry and Voldemort inadvertently created a seventh Horcrux, one that he does not know about. In transferring a portion of himself to Harry, Voldemort has given Harry power that Harry would not have otherwise had. But that power comes with a price; it produces a painful link between the two. When Voldemort is near, angry or violent, the searing pain blinds Harry. This creates a paradox for Harry. Voldemort cannot be killed unless all the Horcruxes are destroyed, thus Harry must die in order for the evil to be removed. He was marked for death from the beginning, and there is no avoiding it. Harry's journey through life, with Dumbledore's guidance, is what prepares him for the moment where he realizes the truth: there is no escaping death. Harry cannot run from Voldemort as that would leave the evil in existence. He cannot overpower him because Harry contains a piece of the evil that Voldemort has become. They are forever linked.

This is the meaning in the prophecy that is the center of action in *The Order of the Phoenix*. As the prophecy stated, "Either must die at the hand of the other for neither can live while the other survives." Initially, the prophecy is interpreted such that one of the two, Harry or Voldemort, must die. However, like most prophecy, the statement is vague and open to interpretation. "Neither can live" tells the truth. Both Harry and Voldemort must die, or both must live, since they are forever linked together. Harry cannot kill Voldemort because the fragment of Voldemort contained in the scar tethers Voldemort to life. If Voldemort kills Harry, destroying the Horcrux in the process, both will face death. Otherwise both will remain alive. The realization of the true meaning in the prophecy is what causes Harry to seek out Voldemort, stand defenseless, and allow Voldemort to kill him. He knows that in doing so, evil will destroy itself.

Yet, Harry is "the boy who survived." He survived the initial attack when he was a baby, and he will survive the attack when he is an adult. Harry does not realize this yet when he offers himself up to Voldemort's attack. He does not realize, although all the clues are there, that Voldemort will only destroy the Horcrux and not end Harry's life. Later he will understand. Murder produces death in the murderer and Harry's survival depends on his voluntarily laying down his life in order that the evil within him will be destroyed. Only through death is the curse destroyed. It is a paradox, but one that tells us how to conquer death. Only those that embrace death can conquer it.

When Voldemort strikes Harry down, it appears that all is lost. Harry wakes up, however, in another place, naked, clean, and renewed. He takes on a new set of clothes, and gains the final understanding that he needs to destroy evil. He sees Voldemort for what he truly is, no longer something to be feared but only pitied. Harry wakes up on the forest floor a new man with the scar he carries no longer painful nor a threat to him. He has conquered death and is renewed with life. He is, as Dumbledore said, the master of death because he did not avoid it.

This paradox is the same one that Jesus spoke of.

> The one who loves his life destroys it, and the one who hates his life in this world guards it for eternal life. If anyone wants to serve me, he must follow me, and where I am, my servant will be too. If anyone serves me, the Father will honor him. Now my soul is greatly distressed. And what should I say? 'Father, deliver me from this hour'? No, but for this very reason I have come to this hour. (John 12:25-27)

Voldemort seeks to save his own life in this world, yet destroys it. The ghosts in Hogwarts were afraid of death, sought to hang on to life, and became shadows never knowing the pleasures of life. Peter Pettigrew sought to protect his life by faking his death, spends many years transformed into a rat, and loses his life in the end anyway. Still, the paradox remains. How can one lose life and save it? The answer to that puzzle is explained by Paul in the epistle to the Romans:

> Or do you not know that as many as were baptized into Christ Jesus were baptized into his death? Therefore we have been buried with him through baptism into death, in order that just as Christ was raised from the dead through the glory of the Father, so we too may live a new life.
>
> For if we have become united with him in the likeness of his death, we will certainly also be united in the likeness of his resurrection. We know that our old man was crucified with him so that the body of sin would no longer dominate us, so that we would no longer be enslaved to sin. (For someone who has died has been freed from sin.)
>
> Now if we died with Christ, we believe that we will also live with him. We know that since Christ has been raised from the dead, he is never going to die again; death no longer has mastery over him. For the death he died, he died to sin once for all, but the life he lives, he lives to God. So you too consider yourselves dead to sin, but alive to God in Christ Jesus. (Romans 6:3-11)

What must die, the Apostle Paul says, is the evil that is within us. We, like Harry, are scarred from sin and that scar must be removed that we might live. We cannot remove it by our own knowledge or power, only by death. What gives us the willingness to accept that death is the promise of a new life that will replace the old. We must be "born again" as Jesus told Nicodemus in the Gospel of John chapter three. When the blood of the one who loved us enough to voluntarily die for us is in us, it provides a protection from evil. Yet, to accept that protection we must throw off the old man, let it die, and be reborn as a new man through the power of the resurrection. The hope of being reborn is what gives us the courage to face death without fear.

That the Christian interpretation is what Rowling intended is made perfectly clear by the inscription on the Potter family tomb: "The last enemy that shall be destroyed is death." That is an exact quote of 1 Corinthians 15:26. The entire fifteenth chapter of the Epistle to the Corinthians speaks of death and resurrection. The one who destroys the enemy is Jesus Christ. Harry is not an allegorical Christ, but clearly he is brought to life through death by a power other than his own. That power is symbolized in the story by sacrificial love that voluntarily lays down its life. That is what Jesus did for us. His sacrifice provides the power that will bring us to life, and thus we do not need to fear death. We follow the footsteps of Jesus, going to death voluntarily for the benefit of another in the sure knowledge of resurrection to come.

Throughout the *Harry Potter* story, evil is associated with self-centered behavior and good with self-denying behavior. This is key to understanding the story, and is key to understanding the Christian gospel. We live not for ourselves, but for another. In dying to self, we gain life. We conquer death through love.

The Postmodern Christian?

Reading through *Harry Potter* I was stunned at the complexity and scope of the saga. If there is any negative criticism I have of the books it is that they are maybe too big, too complex. When I was studying music composition the professors would lecture us on "economy of means" and "thematic development." When artists speak of "economy of means" they mean that you should attempt to get the greatest impact with the smallest amount of material. Choose one theme, in other words, and fully explore that theme, eliminating any extraneous material that does not either express the theme or support it in some way. In part, that means to choose one form, one subject, one technique, and stick with it from beginning to end. Likewise, the artist is expected to be concise so that the theme comes through clearly, not buried among many other elements. That's what any teacher of the arts will tell the students, and what art critics are usually looking for. Economy of means applies equally to music, painting, sculpture, photography, dance, architecture, and literature.

J. K. Rowling has almost thrown that idea out the window. She has created a massive literary work that incorporates multiple literary archetypes and forms, and explores several major and minor themes simultaneously. There are three main characters, many secondary but very significant characters, and many more minor characters that play small but important roles. There are dozens of inventive magical devices, spells and potions that are important to remember in order to follow the plot. It is necessary to remember the invented history of Hogwarts and Harry's world in order to understand the conflicts in the story. All of that together makes it difficult to keep track of everything as you read. There is one major dramatic arc that covers the entire series, but each episode contains its own worked-out plot, with numerous sub-plots, minor conflicts and secondary themes woven in as well. The plot does hold together, however, and everything important is setup with ample foreshadowing. In terms of form and genre, Rowling has taken the 19th century English schoolboy story, blended it with satire, murder mystery, realistic fiction and fantasy to create something that should not work. Yet, it does work. Somehow, she makes it believable.

I don't know whether to call that insanity or genius. Well, maybe it doesn't matter. As my music composition teacher said, "It doesn't matter what you do or how you do it so long as it sounds good." I suppose we could say the same about *Harry Potter*. It doesn't matter that Rowling breaks practically every "rule" of creative writing so long as the story is entertaining to read. *Harry Potter* is certainly entertaining to read, as the huge sales of the books prove.

This complexity is one of the reasons there is so much argument over the books. Had Rowling chosen one clear theme, one literary form, and used more concise narrative, everyone could at least come to an agreement as to what the book was about. As written, there is the possibility that each critic will pick one or two elements to concentrate on and declare those elements as the meaning and intent of the books. Another critic can choose a different part of the story and come to nearly opposite conclusions. This is precisely why teachers of the arts tell students to use "economy of means" and not write the way Rowling does. Yet, I cannot imagine the story any way other than as it was written. Even though I can objectively critique the writing and find things that are normally considered "wrong," the story just seems "right" exactly the way it is. By the end of the story, everything falls into place and every part of the story works together to create a remarkable experience for the reader.

Every artist, no matter what the medium, the historical period or cultural context, will express the times and place he lives in. The artist lives within a society, becomes acculturated by that society, and must inevitably reflect that society and its world view. Even an artist that goes against the norms does this at some level. Consequently, we can look at *Harry Potter* not only as entertaining literature, but also as a reflection of the world we live in.

Artists in Western societies will often seek a new aesthetic ideal or new form of expression in order to be able to express something about the world the artist lives in. One artistic movement follows another, each rejecting the old at least in part. That is something almost unique about Western Civilization since the middle ages. For most human societies, the artist is expected to uphold tradition and avoid wild invention. The arts are considered too crucial to the stability of religion, politics, and society to allow excessive experimentation. That view of art was discarded several centuries ago in the West and since that time we have had one artistic movement after another.

When I was studying music composition during the 1970's and 1980's we had come to the end of the *avant garde* movement. In the preceding decades artists had become so outrageous and conceptual in an attempt to avoid traditional forms that there was nothing left to do. Once someone had burned a piano and called it music there really wasn't anything more outrageous to be done. So, we became "postmodern" artists, rejecting the idea of rejecting traditional forms. The aesthetic that I and others began to explore was how to revitalize what was old within a contemporary culture. Of course, I didn't know it was called "postmodern" at the time. I was just doing what seemed interesting to me. The postmodern ideal results in art that is eclectic, using collage, mixed media, and often paradoxical juxtaposition of forms. Popular forms are combined with "serious" forms, rejecting the distinction between "low art" and "high art."

This seems to be the problem of postmodern writing for many readers. It doesn't fit into preconceived analytical categories, but overlaps many. It "recontextualizes" the traditional, combines opposites into a paradoxical anti-metanarrative and in so doing expresses the metanarrative of the contemporary world view. We seek to include not to exclude, and to recognize the importance of the individual not demand conformity. Postmodernism is a rejection of the modernist hyper-rational rejection of tradition and "superstition." However, the postmodern view is not a Hegelian synthesis, or even an antithesis to the modern, but a rejection of the need for synthesis, a view that embraces paradoxical diversity as the most accurate expression of human existence.

At first glance, Rowling's writing seems to be yet another variation of that postmodern eclectic approach to art. Then again, maybe not. Rowling's *Harry Potter* is possibly an example of the arts moving past postmodernism into something new. We may not have a name for it yet, and this aesthetic may develop further before it is identified as something unique, but I see it as something different from just postmodern eclecticism. It does represent the world we live in. There is a longing for stability, but not through a reactionary movement. The world is new, reinvented every few years with technology, yet there is an appreciation for the personal craftsmanship of past eras. We want to hold the best of the past, but at the same time avoid the isolation of segments of society based on prejudicial attitudes. The contemporary western view of society is "inclusionary" and values diversity, not conformity. However, religion has become isolated from public life and many people would like that isolation to end. The goal is not a theocracy but a return to acceptance of the importance of spirituality in man's life. The arts will reflect all of this.

Harry Potter has that oft-confusing, postmodern eclectic blend. Is it "occultic" or just a parody of magic? Is it secular or Christian in its themes? Is it just a "fantasy story" or an attempt to glamorize the occult? One possible answer is that *Harry Potter* presents traditional Christian themes in a contemporary secular context, but one that is expressed as an eclectic fantasy world not realistically. Since young people are fascinated with the fantastical worlds of medieval romances why not use that form of story telling to get the ideas across? I have no problem with that, at all. *Harry Potter* is not an explicitly Christian novel, but it does embody ideals that are clearly Christian. It is an entertaining story, but is also a moral tale. For those who still have a problem with the form of the writing, consider this: Would Rowling's story have been as well received and widely read had it been yet another pedantic, didactic "Christian" novel? I doubt it. As C. S. Lewis realized, "any amount of theology can now be smuggled into people's minds under cover of romance without their knowing it."[1]

Lewis's statement was a sarcastic response to the failure of critics to see the Christian themes in *Out of the Silent Planet*, but it turns out to be a bit of prognostication as well. We have reached a strange point in Western History. Although Christianity has been the foundation of Western Civilization for 1700 years, today Christianity is identified in the minds of many people with a certain religious observance only. If you don't look like a Christian, then you must

---

[1] Warren H. Lewis ed., *Letters of C. S. Lewis.* New York: Harcourt Brace & World, 1966.

not be one is the attitude of far too many people. Likewise, many will not listen to a Christian teacher because they think of Christianity as a religious form and tradition only. If you strip the religiosity away they cannot recognize the doctrines as Christian. That's what we have in the *Harry Potter* debate. Non-Christians think it is just a fantasy story, while conservative evangelicals think it is a wicked attempt to influence young minds towards a secular, non-Christian world view. In both cases, however, the opinions are based only on the outward appearance and not the imbedded theology of the book. It's the same frustrating problem C. S. Lewis complained about.

It is also the ultimate irony. Because the outward form does not appear to represent traditional religion, non-Christian readers will accept, and even embrace the Christian ideas in *Harry Potter*, even to the point of being upset if you point out to them that the book expresses a Christian world view. The Christian anti-Potter critics reject the clearly Christian nature of the books because the Christian ideas do not have the "proper" and expected outward appearance.

Religion, especially Christianity, Judaism and Islam, seen as something that demands conformity of action and appearance to a traditional norm, is considered by many to be at odds with the postmodern world view. Many people today, especially young people, accept Christianity as one possible private religion, but do not see its doctrines as an all-encompassing explanation for life. Consequently, in public affairs, Christianity is pushed aside, often treated as the crazy old Aunt in the basement that should not be spoken of publicly, much less taken seriously (e.g. *The Humanist Manifesto)*. In other words, a Christian world-view is no longer allowed to act as a foundation for morality or public policy. When evangelicals screech and yell and condemn all non-conformed behavior, their words are ignored as out-of-date, reactionary fundamentalism. This presents a real problem for Christian teachers. How can we get across the "fundamentals" of Christianity to a world that no longer thinks there are universal fundamentals? Answer: we smuggle it in.

What I find most remarkable and exciting about *Harry Potter* is that it truly vindicates the Christian world view. Readers of all ages have accepted, even embraced, *Harry Potter* as a "good" book without even realizing the philosophical and theological foundation for the moral themes expressed in the books. In other words, they accept the ideal that voluntary self-sacrificing love provides protection from evil. They find that embracing death to overcome death based on the hope of a future after-life is the only solution to the paradox of life and death. They likewise recognize the character of evil as something parasitic, prideful and destructive, not a dualistic, opposite but necessary, of the good. *Harry Potter* may not look like traditional Christianity, but its moral themes are about as Christian as you can get. Thus the irony: when stripped of the appearance of religion, the world-view and *a priori* premises of Christianity are readily accepted and embraced even by a postmodern society. And, that is vindication, not denial, of the universal, timeless nature of the Christian message.

www.ingramcontent.com/pod-product-compliance
Lightning Source LLC
Chambersburg PA
CBHW030148200626
46812CB00015B/1744